"An authentic, heartwarming book written with sensitivity and a dash of humor by an author who is herself a military wife."

—ANNA SWENSON,
Author of *Beginning with Braille: Firsthand Experiences with a Balanced Approach to Literacy.*

"In *Married to the Military*, the author's characters are so real that each one will touch your heart. If you are a military spouse, you will know these women; if not, you will gain insight into the diverse but unified roles and lives of military wives. A wonderful book—I couldn't put it down!"

—BARBARA JO RATTÉ,
military wife of twenty-two years to Captain
Paul S. Ratté, US Coast Guard

Married TO THE
MILITARY

To Faye ~

Hope you enjoy the book
and it brings back some
fond memories!

Best Wishes
Always ~

Terry
Nov 2009

TERRY *L.* ROLLINS

Married TO THE MILITARY

*a short story collection sharing
the everyday joys & struggles of military wives*

TATE PUBLISHING & *Enterprises*

Published by Tate Publishing & Enterprises, LLC
127 E. Trade Center Terrace | Mustang, Oklahoma 73064 USA
1.888.361.9473 | www.tatepublishing.com

Tate Publishing is committed to excellence in the publishing industry. The company reflects the philosophy established by the founders, based on Psalm 68:11,
"The Lord gave the word and great was the company of those who published it."

Book design copyright © 2008 by Tate Publishing, LLC. All rights reserved.
Cover & Interior design by Kellie Southerland

Published in the United States of America
ISBN: 978-1-60696-893-2
1. Fiction: Short Stories
2. Fiction: War & Military
08.12.12

DEDICATION

This book is dedicated to four of the important women in my life. First is my mother-in-law, Regina Rollins, who has lived the last fifty-two years as a military wife with style and grace. Next are my two closest coast guard friends, both of whom I have known for over twenty years, Jill Lundstrom and Linda Rieksts. And finally is my mother, Martha McLeese, who has been a constant source of encouragement, always believing in me even when I didn't believe in myself. Thank you one and all.

Contents

Introduction

Being a military wife for the past twenty-three years has been an exceptional experience. It has pushed me to go farther and do more than I ever imagined that I could. It has caused me to know firsthand what it means to be filled with patriotism, pride, and fear, sometimes all in the same day. It has taught me patience, resilience, and humility. But most of all it showed me that being dedicated to one man, in support of his choice to serve the country that we both love, not only helped him and our children but made me a better wife, mother, and American in the process.

For me, being a military wife means understanding that the sacrifices I am making aren't just for the good of my husband, my children, or even myself, but for the greater good of our country, for our freedoms and our future as a nation.

Every military family is a small part of the fabric of what makes our country great. I wrote this book and created these women in the hopes that anyone who reads it will come away with a greater appreciation for the incredibly important contribution military wives make every day, in a million different ways, in places all around the world.

May God bless you and your family, our brave men and women in uniform, their families, our nation, and all of us who continue to be … married to the military.

Terry L. Rollins

Tracy
PREGNANT AND HOSTING
A DINNER PARTY

My name is Tracy, and I'm a military wife. I'm also eight and a half months pregnant with our fourth child. My husband is a C-130 pilot in the coast guard. Between standing duty, flying search and rescue, and rotating out for law enforcement and fisheries patrol for two weeks out of every six, I'm amazed that he's been around enough for us to have even conceived four kids.

Today is a typical day, hectic but typical. The alarm goes off way too early, and I'm still way too tired. My husband, Roger, was up hours ago and is already at work getting his morning brief. I drag myself and this little ten-pound watermelon I've been carrying around out of bed into the bathroom, and my day has begun. I'm running behind, so I rush to wake up my daughter who is in a play at school today and can't be late. I tell her to put on the clothes that we laid out last night. She says okay, but she's got that look on her face like she's plotting something. I'm wondering what it is as I go to wake up our three-year-old daughter and our one-year-old son. After getting the two little ones changed and dressed, we make it to the kitchen for a quick breakfast. I'm watching the clock and calling for my kindergartener to hurry up. She presents herself in the kitchen, and I don't know whether to laugh or cry.

She has definitely changed her outfit from the one we picked out last night, and she's just this side of looking like a miniature call girl! The turtleneck and her church shoes have made it, but somewhere along the way, her conservative little jumper and her tights have given way to bare legs and a pair of shorts that are so tight they look like they could fit her three-year-old sister.

"How do I look?"

I bite my lip, stifle the urge to tell her, "Like all you need is a corner!" and hustle her back into the bedroom telling myself that surely her taste in clothes will improve by the time she's fifteen.

I manage to get everyone loaded into the car—two car seats and a booster—and slide my ever-expanding tummy behind the wheel. Traffic on the base is busier than usual; it's pay day just before a long weekend, and it seems like everyone is out and about. I get our daughter to school just as the bell is ringing and shove her out of the car with promises that I wouldn't miss her play for anything. I drop the little ones off at the base daycare and glance at a notice on the door that says two of the children in the daycare have been sent home with lice in the last week. Great, just what I need. I check my watch and make a mental note to buy RID just in case, and I head off to the commissary to do my grocery shopping.

I grab a cart hoping that for once, all four wheels will be heading the same way, and I'll actually be able to push it in the direction that I want it to go. I check my list for the items I still need for the small dinner party we're having tonight. I still can't believe that the date for Samantha's play was changed to the same day of the dinner party, which has been planned for over a month.

There's no way to change it; it took an act of congress and a hundred phone calls to find a night when all four couples in Roger's office were able to make it. So I resign myself to the fact that I have to squeeze a school play somewhere in between making lasagna, cleaning the house (and anyone with kids knows you can't clean the day ahead because it will just get messed up in the interim and you end up cleaning it twice), and trying to make myself presentable two weeks away from my due date. Roger has said that he only has a two-hour training flight and will try to make it home in the afternoon to help me, but I'm not holding my breath.

I rush home, put the groceries away, and try to ignore the dull pain in my back and my swollen feet. I throw the lasagna together, trying to do justice to my grandmother's sacred recipe, while keeping one eye on the clock. I don't want to get to the school too late because then I'll have to park a half a mile away, and waddling that far is not an option. I decide I have just enough time to set my table and write a "to do" list for Roger when he gets home. If he finishes cleaning the bathrooms, chops the vegetables for the salad, and butters the garlic bread, we might just make it.

I arrive at the school just fifteen minutes before show time, but fate is kind to me, as I am able to slide into a spot near the front that has just been vacated by a harried looking junior officer who has his cell phone in one hand and pager in the other. I file into the school with the other military families, mostly moms, and find a seat on the end of an aisle so I can stretch out my aching feet. For the first time all morning, I am able to relax for a minute and nod and wave to some of the other mothers that I know. That's one of the nice things about living on base; you know a lot of people, if not by name, then by face.

The play is cute, the singing is off-key, and at least a third of the kids spend the whole time waving to their parents who happily wave right back. It's as cute as all kindergarten plays should be, and I find myself wishing, not for the first time, that Roger hadn't missed this little piece of his daughter's history. Luckily, Samantha already understands at the age of five that Daddy has to fly sometimes and can't always be around, even though he wants to be. It's okay. I'm proud enough for both of us, and I give her a big hug and tell her how well she did. She skips off, and I come back to the world of reality and start to think of my dinner party again.

I have just enough time left to pick up the flowers and the wine, stop by the post office to mail an anniversary card to Roger's parents, and pick up his service dress blues from the cleaners. I head down my street thinking that I might actually have time for a bubble bath, when I turn the corner and realize that Roger's car isn't in the driveway. I'm not really surprised: I understand that whenever he takes off in an airplane, even if it's just for a two-hour trainer, there's always the chance that he'll get diverted on SAR (search and rescue) or break down and have to land somewhere and RON (remain over night). But I was hoping just this once that he'd be able to make it home to help me.

This definitely eliminates any chance for a relaxing bath, and I can feel myself approaching just this side of angry. I walk in the door to find the answering machine blinking that I have three messages, none of which are good news, I'm sure. I set the flowers in the center of the table and tell myself that whatever else happens tonight, at least my table will look good.

The first message is just what I suspected. It's Petty Officer Johnson calling to let me know that Roger was diverted on SAR, but that he said to be sure and let me know he thinks he'll make it home in time for the dinner party. I look around the house and suddenly feel very tired. The second message is from my friend Joanie, who has called to tell me that her husband has been called in to fly on the same mission that has delayed Roger and that one of her kids has the flu. She can't find a sitter, so they won't be able to make it. She sounds frustrated and says she was looking forward to a night out with some adult conversation and a meal she didn't have to cook or clean up. However, duty calls and she's homebound for the night. I'm disappointed too, but it goes with the territory. The third message is from the wife of another couple coming tonight who says that her sister has popped in unexpectedly and wants to know if she can bring her... Oh, and she's a vegetarian! For the second time today, I don't know whether to laugh or cry. For the moment I decide it takes way too much time and energy to cry, so instead I decide to start chopping vegetables for the salad.

As I'm standing here asking myself why I ever agreed to host this stupid dinner party so close to my due date, Roger comes flying in the door with his flight suit still on and a look on his face that lets me know he knows he's in the doghouse. As he begins his litany of apologies, I hold up my hand for him to stop. "I warn you right now, Roger, I'm very tired, very pregnant, very hormonal, and I have a knife in my hand. So think very carefully before you speak... And make it good."

He apologizes and tells me he's home now and will do whatever I need him to do. I take him at his word and start barking out orders like a drill sergeant, and he starts running around the house like a first-year swab at the academy. (You have to remember that this is our fourth child, and he knows better than to argue with me in my delicate condition.) I finish the rest of the meal while he picks up the living room, transfers the clean but unfolded clothes from the couch to our daughter's room and closes her door, then vacuums the rug and cleans one of two bathrooms (he must really feel bad because he hates scrubbing the toilet). He is headed for the second bathroom when I decide to grant him a reprieve.

I tell him it's almost time to pick up the kids, so he better hop in the shower. He looks enormously relieved and heads off for the other bathroom. I look around and double-check my list. The house is clean, with the exception of the second bathroom, the food is ready, and the table is set. All that's left is for me to do is get myself ready and for Roger to take the kids to the sitter's. Just as I am about to step into the shower in all my eight and a half months' naked glory, the phone rings, and who should it be but my mother-in-law. If it had been anyone else, including my husband's commanding officer or the president of the United States, I would have politely explained that I was preparing for a dinner party and now wasn't a convenient time to chat. But I know better than to try this with my mother-in-law or I'll never hear the end of it. So I stand there as precious minutes tick by, and my anxiety level is rising by the second. To make matters worse, she has called to brag yet again about Roger's twin brother, who wasn't "foolish enough to waste his potential on a life in the military." Apparently Randall has made partner in his law firm, and she has called to gloat. Ten very long minutes later, I am still buck naked except for my shower cap, having rolled my eyes so many times at my mother-in-law's monologue I've given myself a headache. Finally, I get her off the phone, throw myself into the shower, and finish curling my hair just as I hear the doorbell ring and our first guests arrive. I look around the bathroom and realize it's a lost cause. I will just have to leave everything as it is and just lock the door behind me as I come out so no one can get in there. I greet our guests, who graciously ignore the fact that I look like the Goodyear blimp dressed in a muumuu, and our evening is off and running. The meal is served, the conversation is lively, and even the vegetarian sister seems happy with her salad and bread. I'm starting to feel pretty pleased with myself when I decide to take a bathroom break.

I go to the bathroom that Roger has cleaned but find that it's already occupied. The baby has been sitting with its head on my bladder all night, and this can't wait. So I decide that I will just open the other door with a bobby pin. As I round the corner to do just that, who do I see coming out of our *uncleaned* bathroom but my husband's boss. I stop dead in my tracks in disbelief, and I feel as though I'm about to have an out of body experience. How could he have gotten in there? I know I locked that door! Suddenly images of my maternity bra tossed over the back of the toilet, my *huge* pregnancy panties dropped right on the floor, which on any given day could double as a two-man pup tent, my makeup scattered everywhere, and Roger's whiskers in the sink come to my mind, and I have to steady myself on the wall as I try to come up with any feeble comment to distract him from the hideous sight he's just been subjected to. I half expect someone to jump out of my bedroom and yell, "Surprise, you're on Candid Camera!" Instead I manage to stammer, "Captain, I'm so sorry that you had to see the bathroom in a mess like that. I didn't have time to clean it. I thought I had locked the door, but I guess I didn't."

He smiles and shrugs it off by saying, "That's okay. That's what our bathroom looks like every day." Since I have been in his home several times and knew that his bathroom was nothing less than qualified to be the first runner up in Better Homes and Gardens, I know he is just being gallant. But I manage to erase that "deer in the headlights" look off my face, apologize again, and say that dessert will be served in just a moment. Right! Just give me a moment to slip into the bathroom and have my nervous breakdown.

I walk into the bathroom, look at my gigantic Pee Wee Herman underpants on the floor, and realize I will never be able to look the man in the face again. Somehow I get through the rest of the evening. I barely wait until the door is closed behind the last guest when I round on Roger and yell, "How could this have happened? How did the captain end up in a dirty bathroom with a door that I know I locked? This is like my worst nightmare!"

Roger tries (unsuccessfully) to help me see the humor in the situation but quickly realizes that given my state of exhaustion and general air of hysteria, it's a hopeless cause. Instead, he wisely kisses me on the tip of the nose and suggests that I go soak in a hot bath while he cleans up.

"Great, I'll just go back into the bathroom and relive the nightmare."

He smiles and says, "Don't worry; I've cleaned up the scene of the crime. Just go in there, relax, and take your time. I'll wait for you to come out, and we'll snuggle."

Thirty minutes later, I am much more relaxed and feeling warm and fuzzy toward Roger. After all, he has been a good sport about helping me and has been full of praise for the success of the dinner party, and suddenly, snuggling sounds like a very nice idea. I'm grateful we had arranged for the kids to stay with the sitter so that we could both sleep in. I open the bathroom door into the bedroom and realize that Roger fought the good fight but definitely lost the battle because he is on his back, snoring long and loud with his mouth hanging wide open. Ahh, tender moments like these. Oh well, we can still snuggle, even if he doesn't know that's what we're doing. I crawl into bed, and he rolls over onto his right side. I curl up beside him with my big tummy pressed against his back. And then as if right on cue, the baby decides to start swimming laps, and I can feel legs and elbows going everywhere. I decide to get as comfortable as possible and just enjoy the show when Roger starts to stir.

He says to me in a sleepy voice, "Honey, could you please move? The baby is kicking me in the back, and it's keeping me up."

I can't believe my ears. I must be dreaming. I get up and out of the bed (which is no easy feat at this stage of the game) and waddle over to Roger's side. I snap on the light sitting on his bedside table, put my hands on my hips, and say, "I *cannot* believe you just said that!"

He sits up suddenly on his elbows, one eye shut because of the light and other only half open, his hair sticking up every which way. (Boy, wouldn't I love to have a camera right now and put *this* picture up in the officers' lounge)

He stammers, "What's the matter? Is something wrong? Did I say something?"

"Yes, you said something! You asked me to move because the baby was kicking you and it was keeping you up!"

I wait for his face to register immediate understanding of the insensitivity of the remark, but instead he just has this dumb, mildly panicked look like I have just asked him to recite Einstein's theory of relativity. I can't believe it.

"You must be joking! How could you say something like that to me? I have been carrying this little linebacker around for the last three months, with his head pressed against my bladder and his feet tap dancing on my ribs, and you have the *nerve* to ask me to move because for five minutes of the last nine months, your baby is squirming and it's keeping *you* up?"

Whether it's self-preservation or an actual realization of the implications of what he has just said, I'm not sure, but light is beginning to dawn on his face. I can see he is scrambling for the right response. "I can't believe I would say such a terrible thing. Are you sure that's what I said?"

"Positive!" I say, unwilling to let him off the hook so easily.

"Well, in that case, sweetheart, you're quite right to be upset. Of course you know that I would carry the baby for you if I could …" (Right.) "Here, dear, let's get you back to bed."

I have a feeling that he is being patronizing, but I am too tired to care and allow him to lead me back around the bed to my side and tuck the covers in around me. I look up at him and realize how cute and silly he looks with his hair mashed flat on one side and sticking all up on the other, in his boxer shorts and black socks that he obviously had been too tired to remember to take off when he went to bed. Suddenly I'm not mad anymore, and, in spite of myself, I smile up at him. He looks relieved that I seem to be over it and smiles back, both of us realizing that we have just gotten through another episode of *Raging Hormones of a Pregnant Woman ... It Could Happen to You.* Roger asks me if there is anything I need, and I say, "No, just come to bed."

We have just curled up and gotten all settled, and I am starting to doze off, when it happens.

"Roger ... ?"

"Hmmm?" he replies, already half asleep.

"Actually, there is something I need ... I need to go to the hospital. My water just broke all over the bed."

Suddenly Roger sits bolt upright. "What? Are you sure? Now?"

"Yes, I'm sure. I don't have any contractions yet, so we have a little time. But since this is my fourth, I don't want to underestimate how quickly this might go."

"You and me both," he says with his eyes wide and fully awake. I think to myself that it's funny that my husband can be in complete control when he is flying no matter how bad the weather is or how difficult the mission, but the minute I go into labor, he's completely out of his element. It's as if he knows that he's supposed to be doing something. However, he's not quite sure what, but he wants to do it right and help me get through this. I see a little bit of fear on his face as he goes through the list of what-ifs in his mind, so I take this moment while I'm still rational and not controlled by pain to pat him and reassure him that everything will be okay, just like it was the last three times. He dresses quickly (good thing he left his socks on) while I ready myself for the trip to the base hospital.

Just as we are getting into the car, I feel the first real contraction hit, and suddenly I remember exactly how painful this whole having a baby thing really is. I learned long ago that it's absolutely impossible to try and explain this type of pain to a man. It's like having cramps. Unless you've had them, you just don't get it. Any man could walk a mile in my pumps and still not know how this feels. No, this is one of those rare experiences reserved only for women, and as the contractions start to intensify, I find myself gripping the collar of Roger's shirt and wishing that *he* was the one having this baby. And I can tell from the look on his face that he's definitely glad he's not!

As we arrive at the hospital and the time comes for me to get out of the car, the contractions are coming harder and faster than in the past, and it occurs to me that maybe I have been slowly dilating all day and that this may be quicker than I thought. The minute we walk in, Roger seems to relax a little. He's in a military hospital where there is rank and order that he's used to and is comfortable with, plus he realizes that he's off the hook as far as having to deliver the baby in the backseat of our car. Being an officer's wife, normally they would have tried to get me a labor room to myself. Apparently, though, it's a busy night, so I have to share a room. At this point I don't really care; I just want to get this over with.

So they get me settled in a bed, hooked up to the appropriate monitors, and get the IV in when I sheepishly tell the nurse that I have to go to the bathroom. She is obviously at the end of a very long shift and is less than pleased with this announcement. But Roger quickly volunteers to help me through what can only be described as a somewhat undignified process at this stage. The minute they put that "one size fits all" gown on you with two itty bitty strings to hold it closed in the back, all modesty is gone anyway, and at this point, I just want to get to a bathroom fast. After that's accomplished and Roger helps me heave myself back onto the bed, the nurse reattaches all the monitors, checks my IV, and tells me that the doctor will be in soon to check my progress. Roger asks who is on call tonight, and we're told it's Colonel Sullivan.

"Great," Roger says, "I just played poker with him last week, and he owes me twenty bucks" Here again, that's one of the advantages of living on base; everybody knows everybody. But that can work against you, too, like when you're at a formal dinner and seated across the table from the same guy who just did your pap smear that afternoon!

By now things are really getting going, and when the doctor comes in, Roger has the good grace not to mention the poker debt. The colonel tells us I'm progressing fine and that everything looks good and it shouldn't be too much longer. He slaps Roger on the back and asks if he wants to bet that twenty dollars he owes him on whether it's a boy or a girl. Roger takes the bait and says he thinks it's a boy.

"Well, that leaves me with thinking it's a girl, so we're on."

I'm starting to get seriously irritable and slightly hysterical at the lack of attention I'm getting from Roger at the moment. I tell him through gritted teeth that I don't care if it's a boy, a girl, or a puppy with long ears and a tail. I'm never doing this again. The doctor smiles, pats me on the knee, and says, "That's what they all say." I glare at him as he leaves the room, and he asks the nurse to bring me some ice chips.

Just as I'm beginning to really start to feel sorry for myself, we become aware of the girl that is sharing my room. She is behind a curtain that divides us, but she sounds very young and scared. For a moment I focus on her pain instead of my own. She doesn't seem to have anyone with her, so when the nurse brings in my ice chips, I ask about her. The nurse replies in a hushed tone that the woman is quite young and this is her first baby. She and her husband had arrived at the base just two weeks earlier, and her husband was unexpectedly shipped out just a week later. She doesn't know anyone here and has called her parents, but they are several hours away. The nurse says that they are trying to let her husband know, but he is out to sea with no hope of returning in time to be with her when she has the baby. She sounds so scared, and I realize how common it is for military wives to give birth to their children so many times without the reassurance and support of their husband right when they need it the most.

My eyes pool up with tears, and I am acutely aware how very lucky I am that Roger has been with me for the birth of each of our children. He squeezes my hand in silent understanding, and I say a quick prayer for this young military wife and make a mental note to look in on her after she has her baby. One of the nice things about being a military wife is that you instantly have something in common with every other military wife that you meet. Since this young wife is new to military life, I have no doubt that some of the older, more seasoned wives will take her under their wing and provide comfort, support, meals, and whatever else she may need until her parents arrive or her husband comes home. And I might be able to be of some help in the weeks to come since this is her first and our babies will be the same age.

By this time the contractions are coming one on top of the other. I tell Roger to let the nurse know that I'm beginning to have the urge to push, and they better come and get me into the delivery room, fast. He runs out to find her, and before I know it, there is a flutter of activity. After one last quick check by the nurse, she says, "Okay, let's get you out of here and get this baby delivered."

Everything is a blur now; I'm alternately biting on my lower lip because of the pain and blowing out short quick breaths to keep from pushing and having this baby in the hall. Roger is quickly outfitted with blue scrubs—booties, cap, and all—and before I know it, we're in the delivery room. This is it, the moment that we have waited for and dreamed about for the last nine months, ever since I rushed home to tell Roger that we were having another baby. He leans down, quietly whispers in my ear that he loves me, and asks if I forgive him for putting me through all this again. I smile and tell him that it's worth all the pain and that I wouldn't have it any other way.

Soon, I'm pushing, Roger is urging me on, and our son makes his entrance into the world. We hear the sound of his voice as he cries for the first time, and I ask the doctor if everything is okay. He assures me that the little guy is fine, healthy, and will make a great pilot some day, just like his dad. Roger beams and jokes to the colonel that he just lost that twenty dollars for the second time. Then, our son is placed into my arms for the first time, and we gaze into his beautiful little face. I realize that what started out as a typical day for a typical military wife has ended up as anything but. I tell our new son that he has just become a cherished part of our little family, that someday he'll understand just what that means, and how lucky he is to be the next generation in a proud American military family.

I'm an American military wife, proud of my family, proud of my husband, and proud of the country he's so blessed to serve—maybe this *is* just a typical day.

Jessica
TILL DEATH DO US PART

I will never forget the day he died. It's a memory that's so strong, I carry it with me every day, everywhere I go. I used to think about that day, going over and over the events in my mind. But now, it's more than a thought or a memory, it's part of me, a part of who I am. I remember for the longest time after the accident feeling like everything was going in slow motion, almost like it was a dream. I could see, but I wasn't really seeing; I could hear, but I wasn't really hearing. I moved through the routine of my day kind of like a person riding a bicycle. You know how to do it, so you just do it without thinking. Before you know it, the task is done and you can't even remember doing it.

His name was Brian, and he was my husband. He was young and handsome, a wonderful husband, a caring father, and my best friend.

I met Brian when I was nineteen years old and working in a bookshop. I have always loved books, and it was a cozy, comfortable place to work. We were never so busy that I felt like I was overwhelmed, but we had enough business to keep me from getting bored. I lived in Albuquerque, New Mexico. I was single, working on my bachelor's degree in English literature, and relatively happy with my life. Then one day, Brian walked into the shop. I noticed him immediately because he was exactly the type of guy I found attractive. He was tall with a nice build, but he wasn't too skinny. I have never liked skinny guys, probably because I'm not particularly thin myself. I'm not really fat, but I'm definitely curvy. He was clean-cut with short, sandy-colored hair, and when he happened to turn and catch me staring at him, he smiled with a perfect set of white, even teeth. Having had braces twice, I'm always noticing people's teeth. He walked over to where I was and asked me a question. I felt myself blushing and had to ask him to repeat himself. I helped him find the book he was looking for and asked him if there was anything else I could help him with.

He smiled again and said, "Yes, you can tell me your name. Mine is Brian."

I normally don't give my name out to just anyone, but for some reason I wasn't worried that time. "Jessica," I told him.

After some polite conversation that gradually became mild flirtation, he said, "Well, Jessica, if you're not married, engaged, or otherwise attached, I wonder if you would feel comfortable having dinner with someone you barely know?"

"That someone being you?"

"None other…" He smiled. I must have looked slightly uncomfortable because he gallantly suggested that I could pick a place that I felt comfortable with, and that if I wanted, we could each drive there so that if I found him horribly boring, I could escape at will. Not only was he good-looking, but he was kind and had a good sense of humor, so I figured he was worth the risk and accepted his offer. An evening with a handsome stranger, even if he was boring, was definitely a better prospect than doing my laundry, which is what I had planned for Friday night.

Thankfully, when we did go out, boring never entered the picture. I couldn't get enough of him, the way he looked, the way he talked—everything about him. I'd never felt so comfortable with anyone before. The hours passed so quickly; we barely even touched our food. I learned that he was the oldest of four boys from Flagstaff, Arizona, and in the air force. He was stationed at Kirtland Air Force Base in Albuquerque. I listened with fascination as he described his lifelong love of flying and how he had gone to college at Northern Arizona University, then officer's training school at Maxwell Air Force Base in Montgomery, Alabama, and then finally to flight school at Fort Rucker, Alabama. Now he was a helicopter pilot going through what he called "night vision training" in Albuquerque. I was impressed with all the places he'd lived so far, and the night vision thing sounded kind of interesting. He talked about it with the excitement of a kid with his first model airplane. His life seemed much more exciting than my quest for my English lit degree, but he seemed genuinely interested when I told him about my dreams of teaching at the college level and maybe even writing a book someday. In fact, he said, he would be the first one in line to buy a copy!

After our first date, we were together almost every day. He had a fairly busy schedule, and most of his training was at night. I worked at the bookshop during the day, but he managed to come and meet me for lunch as often as he could. I found myself watching the clock all morning, eagerly waiting for my break. One day he showed up with a picnic basket and asked me to lead him to the nearest park, and we had a wonderful afternoon. The weather was perfect, and he even convinced me to take the rest of the day off and spend it with him. I never would have done that before, but suddenly, being with Brian was the only thing that mattered. We talked about everything—our childhoods, our families, what we wanted out of life—and the more we talked, the more we realized how much we had in common. I couldn't believe that this guy was for real and that he just walked into my life one day and everything changed, just like that. Everything we did was better because we did it together. Every time he kissed me, it was as if we were the only two people in the world; everything else just melted away. Suddenly even my desire to pursue my degree seemed less important to me if it meant I would have to be away from Brian.

Many years later, one of our children asked me when I knew I was in love with their daddy. The answer was easy. It was after we'd been dating for almost two months, when he invited me out to the base to watch him fly. I had never been on a military base before since I didn't come from a military family, so for me it was really exciting. We went through a guard gate where Brian had to show his military ID, and since there was a sign that said 100% ID Check, I had to show them my driver's license too. I remember thinking, the MP, as I learned later he was called, was very serious looking and that I felt a little intimidated. Brian of course was perfectly at ease. His dad and two of his brothers are in the military also, so he was raised on bases.

He took me around and showed me the various areas of the base: the commissary (grocery store), the BX (base department store), the Class Six store (liquor store), the base hospital, and the various hangars that housed more airplanes and helicopters than I'd ever seen in one place before. It seemed like there were a lot of barbed wire fences around and a lot of security. Finally we pulled into a spot in front of a building that said "Flight Operations," and Brian started to introduce me. Everyone I met was very friendly, and most of the guys (and two women) had on flight suits. Brian had tried to explain the rank system to me, but I could tell after the introductions that I was going to have to go home and study it a little more before it would make sense. Brian was an air force captain at the time, that much I knew.

We went into the operations center, where there were big maps on the walls, a lot of instruments, and phones, and one whole wall was a window that faced out onto the "tarmac." Brian left me in the company of the current duty officer, checked his flight schedule, and returned a few minutes later in his flight suit, carrying his helmet. It was the first time I'd seen him dressed like this, and suddenly, the fact that he was a pilot seemed very real. I got this funny feeling in my stomach. He informed me that he was doing a check flight on a helicopter that had just had some maintenance done on it, so he would be doing take-offs, hovering, and landings. He said I should be able to see everything from the window.

"It seems kind of windy to me. Are you sure this is okay?" I asked him.

He just kind of chuckled and said, "Yes, I'm sure it's okay, or we wouldn't be doing it. If we have to do a rescue, we have to be prepared to fly in any kind of weather, and we are. Although you're right, we generally don't do test flights if the weather is bad."

I think he was pleased that I was worried about him. As he went over the recent repairs and the flight plan with his co-pilot, my palms began to sweat, and I realized just how much I did care. What was obviously routine for Brian was anything but for me, and I began to wonder if my watching him was such a good idea. He gave me a quick kiss and told me to enjoy the show and that he'd be back before I knew it. When he walked over to that helicopter, climbed in, and a few minutes later brought it roaring to life, I knew that the clutch in my heart was a fear that something would happen to him, and that if it did, I couldn't bear it. That's when I realized I loved him. And what I never could have known when I watched him fly on that very first day was how right I was to be afraid.

Before I knew it, Brian's training was coming to an end, and he would soon be getting his orders to his permanent duty station. We'd both known for a while that we never wanted to be apart. One evening he took me for a drive into the foothills around Albuquerque, and we watched the sunset. He pulled out a beautiful ring and asked me how I felt about becoming a military wife. I didn't know anything about what it meant to be a military wife, but I knew without a doubt that I wanted to be Brian's wife. We talked about the kind of life that we would lead with frequent moves, deployments, possible overseas assignments, and the distinct possibility of living in less-than-glamorous base housing. He was trying to be fair and warn me that the life of a military wife wasn't always easy. I suppose that someone less naïve would have given the idea of long deployments and being alone so much some serious thought. I just kept telling myself that nothing he said or could say could keep me from wanting a life with him, no matter what hardships that might include. To me it was all an adventure. And so our life together officially began.

We informed our parents, of course, and Brian's were thrilled. Since he was the oldest and first to be married in a house full of boys, I was the first daughter, and they welcomed me with open arms. My parents liked Brian but were a little less excited about the prospect of me giving up working on my degree and moving to places unknown. I think they just always assumed that I would meet some nice boy there in Albuquerque, and they would always have instant access to their future grandchildren. But when I explained how happy we were and how much I loved him, they knew that there wasn't much they could do and gave us their blessing.

Right about that time, Brian received his orders to Little Rock, Arkansas, and we decided to have a quiet wedding in a little chapel on the base at Kirtland. Both of our families were there, all of Brian's brothers and my sister. He had asked several of the guys that he knew from training to come, and as we left the chapel, they made an arch with their swords. Brian stopped just before we passed under it and gave me a kiss, telling me it was good luck. And I did feel lucky and blessed, and I couldn't wait for our future together.

The next few years flew by. We were at the base in Little Rock for three years, and we had two children by the time we left to go overseas to a base located in the United Kingdom. It was a busy, happy time. I loved England, and we traveled as often as Brian's schedule would allow. He was with a special operations command, and he was gone quite a bit. But he had warned me this would happen, so I kept myself busy with our two girls, taking them back and forth to pre-school and daycare, making cupcakes, having birthday parties, and doing the mom thing.

Being a military wife wasn't too hard. He was right about the base housing; it had noisy pipes and antiquated appliances in the kitchen. But it had a great backyard that the girls loved to play in, and I had already made friends with some of the other wives in Brian's squadron. Whenever the guys were gone, we would all get together and keep each other company, watch each other's kids, swap recipes, and complain about how often our husbands were gone. It was a little hard being so far away from my parents in New Mexico, but we spoke on the phone at least once a week. My sister was great at writing me every couple of weeks and sending pictures of any family events I missed. Sometimes though, the base felt like a fishbowl. It was hard to have any privacy because everyone could see when you were coming and going, and if it was a nice day and the windows were open, it was easy to tell if someone was having a bad day since you could easily hear raised voices. All in all though, I was happy to be living on base;

I felt safe there, and everything was located so nearby that many times I took the girls out in their stroller instead of the car if we needed to run errands.

Always though, my thoughts were with Brian. I worried constantly about the dangers he faced every day as a pilot. By that time, I knew the risks involved and had heard enough horror stories from the more seasoned pilot wives to give me nightmares for a month. I knew that Brian was a good pilot and that he never took chances, but sometimes I wished he was in another line of work. I remember asking him about it one summer day.

We had taken a picnic to a nearby old English castle that had a huge expanse of yard. The girls had been running and playing with Brian all day, and both had fallen asleep on the blanket we had put under a tree. So for the moment, all was blissfully quiet. I asked Brian if he had ever considered getting out of the air force and trying something else. He was chewing on a blade of grass and shook his head back and forth. "No, I'm a career officer. The military life is in my blood, and I'll be here ready to serve as long as they'll have me. It's more than just a job to me, Jess; it's the whole idea about what it means to be a part of the greatest military force on the earth, serving and protecting the greatest country in the world. It may sound corny, but it means something to me when I think about all the men who have come before us, who fought and died so we could enjoy all the freedoms and security that we do. So many people forget that and take it for granted."

"Sure, I could go out and chase the almighty buck, and we'd probably live in a nice house and wouldn't have to move like we do. All of that would be great. But it's not who I am, and I wouldn't be living what I believe. Next to you and the girls, the most important thing to me is my honor and integrity, and if I left the serving and defending of this country up to 'the other guy,' then I don't think I would feel like I had either, no matter how successful I was in another job. My dad always used to tell me that a person can't be more or less than what they are, so I better be sure that the man I become is the man I want to be. And this is who I am. Does that make any sense?"

I remember telling him that it made perfect sense. Some people are moved to tears every time they sing the national anthem because it means so much more than just the song, and for others, it's only words and music before the ball game. I knew at that moment that no matter what hardships the future might bring, I would never regret a moment of it because Brian was living the life he was born to live. It wasn't just a job; it was a part of him.

The years continued to fly by. We moved three more times and added one more little girl to our family. I was afraid that Brian might be disappointed that we didn't have a boy, but he always assured me that he was raised with nothing but boys and that he was thrilled with his little blond-haired, blue-eyed girls. And every day he made them feel it. He was never too busy to read to them, listen to their stories, or take them to the park to fly their kites. He realized that the amount of time that he was gone was hard on the girls, and he did his best to make up for it every time he was home. I really couldn't have asked for anything more. They adored him, almost as much as I did.

We'd been married for almost thirteen years, and we were living in Anchorage, Alaska. Alaska is one of the most beautiful states in our country, and we all fell in love with it as soon as we got there. We would take drives on Sundays and try to spot eagles who sometimes built their massive nests on the side of the road. Brian taught the girls how to fish, and he explained to them how the salmon would come back to spawn every year at the exact place where they were born. They used to love watching them struggle so hard against the stream just to get home again. We even enjoyed the Alaska winters. It would be dark by four o'clock in the afternoon and wouldn't be light again until about ten o'clock the next morning. For some people, this was agony because they felt so sun deprived. But it was always fun for us. The girls would help me make bread and big pots of stew, and we would light a fire in the fireplace and wait for Brian to come home. Some evenings, when the wind was howling and the snow was blowing sideways, we would stay snuggled up in front of the fire and play board games, read, or play charades. The weather was the only thing that really worried me about our life in Anchorage, and that was only because at times the conditions made for some of the worst and most challenging flying in the world. Of course Brian loved it. He always used to say it was the best duty station he ever had because the challenges of flying in that type of environment made him the best pilot he could be.

Brian was an excellent pilot with a natural skill, and I knew more than one of the other guys that flew with him admired him. But even the most skilled of pilots was no match for Mother Nature in Alaska when she reared her ugly head. And that's just what she did one cold day in November.

It had been a fairly typical day; we had gone to church even though the weather was bad, and since we had all been up late the night before, we decided to take a nap. I put the roast in the oven, the girls went off to their rooms to read or sleep, and I curled up next to Brian and listened to the wind howling outside our bedroom window. I told him that I wished he didn't have duty that night. I hated him being on call when the weather was like this. He said that he probably wouldn't get called and that hopefully even the fishermen they were sometimes called on to rescue were safe at home too. We enjoyed a quiet afternoon together, talking about our upcoming vacation over the Christmas holiday. Our plans were to take the girls to Disneyland in California, fly on to my parents' house for Christmas, and then to Brian's parents' house in Flagstaff for a New Year's family reunion. We were both really excited and ready for a break from the winter weather.

After a short nap, I slipped off the bed, went to get the roast out of the oven, and set the table. I noticed that it was starting to sleet, and I said a silent prayer that Brian wouldn't get called to fly. I had no idea in those moments that I had just laid in bed with my husband for the last time, that I would never be able to call him to dinner again, and that we would never hold hands and pray as a family again. Just as we began to eat, Brian's beeper went off. I couldn't believe it. Even the girls were a little concerned as they looked at the sleet pounding at our dining room windows.

"Gosh, Daddy, they won't make you fly with the weather like this, will they?" our oldest asked. He assured us that they wouldn't fly if it wasn't safe and that he'd be extra careful if they did. He tweaked our youngest daughter on the nose and asked them to be sure to save him some dessert, as he would be back before they knew it. He turned to me with an apologetic smile and asked me to put his plate in the fridge. He said he would warm it up when he got back, which he hoped wouldn't be too long. Suddenly I wasn't very hungry, and I told him that I would wait and eat with him, even if he got in late. He pulled me into the kitchen, gave me a warm embrace, and whispered in my ear that he thanked God every day that he walked into that bookstore that day and that marrying me was the best thing that ever happened to him. He whispered that as soon as he got home, he planned on showing me just how happy he was. I smiled and told him to hold that thought and just get home safely. "Always," he said. He put his flight suit on, grabbed his gear, and then kissed each of the girls good-bye. I walked him to the door and hugged him one last time. I remember as he reached for the doorknob, he turned for a moment and winked at me. Then he opened the door and ran out into the sleet to his truck. He gave me a quick little wave and drove away.

For the remainder of the evening, I tried to keep myself occupied while waiting to hear from Brian as to whether he was really going to launch in this weather. He always tried to call before he went out to let me know for sure he was going and when he might be back. About an hour and a half after he left, the phone rang, and I ran to pick it up. It was Brian, and he said that they had a medical evacuation inland about 250 miles away. A man had gotten drunk, fallen, and impaled himself on a fence post. They had called in the base doctor, a physician's assistant, and a medical tech, all of whom were also on duty like Brian, meaning they only went into work if there was a search and rescue or, in their case, a medical evacuation. I protested about the weather, but he said they had been watching it for the last hour. They thought they saw a break in the pattern, so they were going to take off. He quietly explained that if he had his choice he'd rather not fly in weather like this either. However, a man's life was at stake, and he would die if they didn't get him to a hospital within the next few hours. I was quiet for a moment, inwardly seething that my husband was going to have to risk his life and the life of everyone on that aircraft because some guy decided to get drunk. Brian already knew what I was thinking and told me that it wasn't his job to make any kind of moral judgment on the circumstances of this mission, but to do it safely and to the best of his ability. I knew he was right, and as usual I respected his integrity when it came to his job. But I was scared and he knew it.

"You'll probably hear us taxi out in about twenty minutes, and we should hopefully be done and back home before morning. I'll have someone at the desk call you when we're on our way back in, okay? So don't worry, just go on to bed and wait for me, and I'll see you in the morning. And tell the girls that I will pick them up from school tomorrow, and we'll go and get ice cream."

I did my best to sound cheerful and told him to be careful and that I'd be listening for him to get back home. He told me he loved me and that he had to go, and then the conversation was over. I slowly hung up the phone, walked over to the window, and put my forehead on the cold glass. The wind was still blowing a combination of snow and sleet almost sideways, and ice was starting to form on our back porch.

"Please, God," I prayed, "please bring him back home."

I managed to make it through our normal nighttime routine with the girls, laying out clothes for school the next day, packing lunches, doing baths, brushing teeth, reading books, and finally getting in bed. For some reason I was craving peace and quiet, so I could just sit, think, and pray. I added another log to our fire, changed into sweatpants and a sweatshirt, and made myself a cup of hot tea. I turned off all the lights in the den except for one small lamp that cast a warm glow across the room and then curled up on the couch to wait.

I looked around at all the familiar objects in the room, which was the heart of our home. I looked up at the stenciling I had so painstakingly done around the top of the walls. Brian had teased me because I had taken it so seriously and was getting so frustrated when it wasn't as perfect as I thought it should be. Beside the fireplace was the beautifully carved bookshelf that Brian had made me for our anniversary a few years ago to hold my collection of favorite books. I had been so touched that he had found the time to make something like that for me, and he even kept it a surprise. I ended up putting some of my favorite pictures of him and the girls that I had taken over the years among my books, and it gave me a very satisfied feeling every time I looked at it.

The room was warm and cozy, and I felt guilty knowing that Brian was out there flying in some of the worst weather we'd had since we moved to Alaska. I don't know how long I sat there staring into the fire, thinking of all the fun times we'd shared in the last thirteen years, but sometime around 2:00 a.m., I decided that I had better go to bed if I had any hope of getting up when the alarm went off and getting the girls to school. I crawled into bed, still straining my ears for the familiar sound of a helicopter taxing back in to the hangar. It was a sound I'd heard a hundred times since our house on the base was so close to the taxi way; I'd just never been as desperate to hear it as I was that night.

The next thing I knew, our radio alarm had gone off. It was 6:30 a.m., and I was waking up slowly to the sound of morning news and weather like always. Still half asleep, I heard the announcer say something about a helicopter having crashed on a mountainside about 230 miles away. Suddenly I was wide awake, looking wildly around the room for Brian. *Oh no… Oh no… he's not back, and they haven't called… Did he say helicopter crash? Oh Lord, please don't let it be… please don't let it be…* I could hear my breath making a short raspy sound. I jumped out of bed to get to the phone and call the operations center so they could tell me this was a private helicopter that had crashed, not an air force one. But I never even made it to the phone because the minute that I ran into the kitchen, I could see our next-door neighbors, Curt and Susan, coming to my back door. The looks on their faces told me everything I needed to know, and I froze right where I was standing and tried to take in the meaning of why they were coming to my house at 6:30 in the morning. I knew what it was, but I refused to accept it. I just stood there making this kind of whimpering sound. I could hear it, but it didn't sound like me; it was like I was listening to someone else. My heart started to pound, I felt my legs go weak, and I started to say to myself, "This isn't happening, this isn't happening…" But it was. As I moved to the door, I felt like I had fifty-pound weights on each leg, and when I opened it, I said in a voice that was barely audible, "Please just tell me he's not dead, please just tell me…"

They moved in quickly and put their arms around me. Curt said immediately, "We don't know anything for sure yet, Jess, only that Brian's helicopter crashed into the side of a mountain around 2:00 a.m., and they've got crews out right now trying to determine if there were any survivors."

I was trying to take in what he had just said to me, and for a moment I couldn't speak. It was all I could do to try and understand what he was telling me. A mountain…survivors…I looked into Curt's face and saw that he was composed but obviously very concerned. Susan's face was probably more of a reflection of mine. She was very pale and was biting on her lower lip, obviously trying not to cry. Curt and Susan were our best friends. We had watched each other's kids, been to one another's houses for dinner and games too many times to count, and had even taken a couple of family vacations together. But now they seemed like strangers, or even enemies, because they were telling me something that I didn't want to hear, that I couldn't let myself believe, because if I believed it, then it was true. I just couldn't let it be true.

They led me into the living room and sat me down on the couch. Curt turned on the lamp while Susan returned to the kitchen to make some hot tea. I still hadn't said a word, and Curt pulled up a chair right across from me and took both of my hands.

"Jessie, do you understand what I told you?"

I looked up and told him that I had heard him. "But how could this have happened? Brian is such a good pilot; he told me that he was going to be careful!"

"He is a good pilot, Jess; I've flown with him and I know

he is. But sometimes things happen that are out of our control, and it can happen to even the best of pilots, especially on a night like last night."

"Are you sure it was them?"

"Yes, we lost communication with them just about the same time someone reported seeing a large flash on a mountain that was very near their flight path."

"And you don't know if there are any survivors?"

"No, they have people flying out there now, but the wreckage is on the side of a mountain. It's difficult to reach, so it may take a little while."

The word *wreckage* brought to my mind a horrific scene, and to think that Brian was out there somewhere, either injured or, at the worst, even dead, on the side of a mountain, was more than I could bear. I crossed my arms over my stomach, clenched my fists, and let the tears come. I couldn't make a sound, my throat was too tight, but the tears came. There was no way to stop them. I closed my eyes, and all I could see was Brian's face as he winked at me the night before when he left. As reality slowly began to sink in, I knew that I had lost him and that my life would never be the same again. It felt as if someone had just stabbed a knife into my heart, and there was no way to take it out or make the pain go away. I couldn't run from it or hide from it. It was just there, and all I could do was to try and bear it one moment and one breath at a time.

Susan brought me the tea, but I shook my head no. There was no way I could get it past the lump in my throat.

"There's still hope, honey; we've just got to pray and keep believing until we get some news," she said.

I looked up at Susan and then at Curt, and I knew by the look on his face that he didn't hold out much hope. And somehow in my heart, I knew he was gone. Brian was gone, and it would only be a matter of time before the chaplain would come to my door and say the words that no wife should ever have to hear, that her husband is dead. Curt asked me if there was anyone I wanted him to call, and I said no, that I wanted to wait until we had something definite to tell our families. Everyone was so far away; they couldn't get here anyway, and there was no reason for them to have to suffer any longer than necessary. Curt excused himself to make some phone calls in Brian's office, and Susan told me to lie down on the couch and then put a cool rag on my forehead. We decided to let the girls sleep in; there was no way we could send them to school, as this was going to be one of the hardest days of their lives. I wanted them to stay unhurt and unaware for as long as possible. Plus, I needed a while to pull myself together so I could be reasonably calm when they did wake up and I had to tell them about their daddy. Their daddy...I couldn't bear the thought of him missing the rest of their lives, their growing up, the birthdays, graduations, and weddings; it would all be different now. I could feel it already, and the tears began to flow again.

As word began to spread around the base about the accident, the phone began to ring with calls from concerned friends. Most of the men had been called into work immediately after the helicopter went missing, and someone in the wives club had already started to arrange meals for the families of the men who had been on board. Since Brian was the aircraft commander and the senior member of the flight crew, I felt some responsibility for the other families whom I knew were suffering as much I was. Susan reassured me that they were being taken care of by friends and that the chaplain was making his rounds. Susan had promised to stay with me as long as I needed her and called another wife to stay with her kids for as long as she was needed at my house. Curt kept busy in Brian's office, fielding calls and staying in constant contact with the operations command center on the progress of the search and rescue effort. Every fifteen minutes or so he would come out, check on me, and ask if there was anything I needed him to do.

Thankfully, in the two hours since Curt and Susan had come to the door, the girls had not woken up, and I was grateful for the time I had alone, knowing that once they woke and realized what was happening, there would be lots of questions and tears. I didn't feel ready to cope with it yet. I realized a little bit later that I would probably never feel ready to cope with it and that it was probably best to go in, wake them up, and tell them what had happened. I went in first to our twelve-year-old, sat down on the side of her bed, and gently began to pat her back to wake her up. She rolled over, looked at me with sleepy eyes, and said, "Hi, Mommy. Is it time to get up?" I told her yes, that I had let her sleep in a little and that she needed to sit up so that I could talk to her. She looked at me a little closer and immediately sensed that something was wrong. "What's the matter with your eyes? You look like you've been crying or something, and your voice sounds funny." I explained as gently as I could that I had been crying because something pretty sad had happened to our family, and before I could even go on, she said, "Oh no, it's Daddy, isn't it? Did he crash? He's not dead, is he?"

"Yes, honey, there was an accident, and they are trying to find out now exactly how bad the accident was and if there are any survivors."

I saw her eyes grow wide as they filled with tears, and she pulled her knees up to her chest like she was trying to protect herself from the pain that I was inflicting on her.

"He can't be dead, Mommy, he just can't … Do you think he's dead?"

I hesitated before I answered her, not knowing whether to be completely honest and tell her the chances weren't good, or to allow her to cling to hope for a little while longer until she was face-to-face with the reality of it. I decided that the pain of finality would be hard enough when it came, so I just told her that I didn't know, that all we could do was pray. But I tried to comfort her by saying that if Daddy was gone, then he was safe in heaven, watching over us from there. She was crying openly, saying that she didn't want him there, she wanted him here, and that she couldn't believe that God would let this happen. Before we could discuss it any further, her younger sisters came into the room and hopped up on the bed.

Our middle daughter, Amy, asked, "What's wrong? Is Megan in trouble or something? Why is she crying?" I pulled the two little ones close and said as calmly as I could that, no, Megan wasn't in trouble, but that I had some very sad news and that they would have to try and be big girls and try to understand.

"What is it?" our youngest daughter, Elizabeth, or Betsy, as we called her, asked with her eyes wide and a frightened look on her face.

I began the task of trying to explain. "Do you remember last night when the weather was so bad, and Daddy got called in to work?" They both nodded and didn't say a word. "Well," I continued, "a man got hurt out in a remote area, and he needed to be taken to a hospital. The only way to get him there in time to try and save his life was by helicopter, so that's why they called Daddy into work, to go and pick up the man."

"Did the man die before Daddy got there?" Amy inquired.

"No, honey, actually, Daddy never made it to the man. Before he could get there, the weather became so bad that they had an accident on the way."

"What happened exactly, Mom?" Megan asked.

I didn't want to tell them the few horrifying facts that I already knew, but they needed to begin to understand the seriousness of the accident. I decided to go ahead and tell them that the helicopter had hit the side of a mountain and that right now we didn't know how many people were hurt or killed.

"Who else was with Dad?" Megan asked.

"Well, do you remember the tall single man with brown hair who helped you guys put up the volleyball net at the welcome picnic a couple months ago?" She nodded, and I continued. "Well, he was Daddy's co-pilot, and the two other members of the crew have very young children. I don't think you know them. And because this was a medical evacuation, Dr. Stephens and two of the medics who work with him at the base clinic were also with them."

Amy looked horrified. "Do you mean the Abby Stephens in my class at school?"

I nodded.

"Well, that's good, isn't it?" asked Betsy. "That way, if Daddy is hurt then there is a doctor who can take care of him, right?" I hugged her close and told her that I was sure that if Dr. Stephens wasn't hurt himself, he would be helping the others who were.

No one spoke for a moment, and then Betsy said in a very small voice, "I hope Daddy's not cold. There was lots of ice and snow last night."

I bit my lip to keep the tears from coming again and allowed myself just for a moment to hope that he *was* cold because that meant that at least he was alive. I told the girls that they wouldn't be going to school that day and that they could go curl up in our bed and watch a video to help keep their minds off things. I told them that I would bring them some breakfast, and I would let them know as soon as I got any more news. I told them that I loved them and that I was proud of them and that Daddy was too.

The next few hours went by painfully slowly. The phone rang several times, and Curt was taking all the calls. Every time I expected it to be some word on Brian. He finally came in and told me that a team of rescuers had been dropped at the base of the mountain, below the crash sight. They were making their way slowly up to it, and they should be there within the next couple of hours. What he didn't tell me at the time was that after multiple passes by another air force rescue chopper, they had seen absolutely no signs of life. The only thing that was visible was a smoldering hunk of twisted metal that used to be a helicopter and debris scattered halfway down the mountainside.

Hours passed like days, and Susan was gently trying to get me to eat something. It had been almost twelve hours since Brian's helicopter had crashed, and I knew that it was in the low 20s on that mountain. Even though I felt in my heart that it would be almost impossible to survive that type of catastrophic crash, I hoped for Brian's sake that if he was alive that he was unconscious and not suffering.

I checked on the girls and decided to take a shower and change clothes since I was still in my pajamas and bathrobe. I slipped quietly into our bathroom and turned the shower on hot. I glanced at my reflection in the mirror and barely registered the pale and gaunt reflection that stared back at me. I was completely alone for the first time since I had learned of the accident, and as I stepped into the privacy of the shower, the full reality of losing Brian hit me. I sank to my knees and cried harder than I had ever cried in my life. The sobs were so deep they shook my entire body, and even drawing breath was hard. I couldn't believe the intensity of the pain that a human being could feel at the loss of a person they loved so much. I knew in that moment that until I drew my last breath on earth, I would never, ever get over this. I'm not sure how long I cried, but when my shower was over, I was calmer. I think that was when the numbness set in and a small part of me just seemed to die. I didn't feel whole anymore, but I knew that from that point on, I had to consider the girls. They were a part of Brian, and I knew that's what he would have wanted.

So an hour and half later, when I was seated at my dining room table wearing jeans and a turtleneck and saw the official car drive up in front of our house, I knew why it was there. Susan sat down beside me, put her arm around me, and told me she was there for me and to hold tight to her if I needed to. Kathy, another friend who was there to deliver a meal, walked back to sit with the girls so they wouldn't come out and hear the news before they were ready. As the wing commander, the CO of Brian's squadron, and the base chaplain, all in their dress uniforms, walked slowly to my door, Curt squeezed my hand and went to let them in. I didn't want them to come in. I didn't want them to tell me he was dead, because then the tiny sliver of hope that I had been clinging to, the hope that he had somehow survived, would be gone forever.

But of course they did come in and told me as gently as they could that the helicopter had crashed into the side of a mountain last night at approximately 2:00 a.m. on its way to a medical evacuation. The rescue teams had arrived at the crash site and determined that there were no survivors. Brian's body had been positively identified and would be arriving back at the base within the next hour. I knew that delivering this type of devastating news to a family member was one of the hardest parts of their job, and I appreciated their level of tact and kindness. I had just lost my husband and the father of my children, but they had lost a part of their tight-knit squadron family. I knew the effects of this went far beyond me and the girls. I asked if they thought everyone had died on impact, and they replied that it appeared that way from what they knew thus far. However, the investigation had only begun, and they would know more about exactly what had happened in the weeks and months to come. I asked them if they had any idea what went wrong, and they hesitated and said that like with most aviation accidents, it probably wasn't any one thing but rather a combination of things that conspired together to bring the aircraft down, not the least of which was the weather.

Brian's squadron commander made a point of telling me that Brian was an outstanding pilot who never took any unnecessary chances and that their decision to fly was considered from every possible angle. As the squadron commander, he had given the go-ahead for the flight to take place, taking into consideration recommendations from all concerned, including the crew, the operations officer, and the maintenance officer. They had all agreed that the weather was bad, but the mission was doable. Considering a man's life was at stake, it was worth the margin of risk. He went on to say that he knew that there was nothing he or anyone could do to ease the pain of our loss, but he wanted me to always remember that Brian was an outstanding young officer who loved what he was doing and that it had been his distinct honor to have served with him. I could tell by the sincerity in his voice and the tears in his eyes that he meant it, and I thanked him. I knew he felt badly and that most commanding officers that lose any of the men under their command take it personally.

The chaplain went on to say that if I could give them a list of people that needed to be notified, they would take care of it for me, and I would have all the help I needed to see to all the arrangements when the time came. If there was anything I needed, all I had to do was ask. Curt let them know that he and Susan would be there for me and the girls for anything we might need. I asked about the other families of the crewmembers and was especially concerned about Dr. Stephens' wife since they had six children. I was assured that the entire military community was already coming together to meet the needs of the families who had lost loved ones.

The chaplain asked if I knew where Brian wanted to be buried, and I said that I would have to discuss it with his parents before I made a decision. We had never discussed it because Brian had always told me that when he died, it was just the shell that would be left behind and that his soul would be in heaven waiting for me. I was hopeful that at some point in the future, the thought that I would see him again one day would be a comfort to me, but for now I had to focus on making it from one moment to the next. I still had two very difficult tasks ahead of me: breaking the news to the girls and telling Brian's parents and his brothers. And that didn't even take into consideration how I was going to make it through the rest of my life without him.

The next few days were some of the most difficult in my life. I don't think I'll ever forget the heart-wrenching cries of the girls when I told them that their daddy was gone. We all just lay on my bed, clung to one another, and cried. Even reassurances that we would see him again one day in heaven did little to ease their pain. I knew that all four of us had a long struggle ahead and that we would just have to take it one day at a time. I know without a doubt, though, that if it hadn't been for the girls, I wouldn't have maintained my sanity for long.

Brian's parents were devastated, of course. I can imagine that the only thing worse than losing a spouse would be losing your child, no matter how old they are. My parents were terribly upset too, and my mother said that she would be on the next plane to Anchorage to help me look after the girls and make the necessary arrangements. I was grateful that she realized immediately how much I needed her.

The wives in the squadron had been wonderful too. They had arranged for meals for us for as long as we needed them and offered to run errands and do anything that needed to be done. They even offered to clean and do laundry, but I declined. I wasn't sure I'd ever wash our sheets again. The only way I had made it through the last two lonely nights in our bed without Brian was to wrap myself around his pillow and breathe in the smell of him.

My mother arrived on the third day and was a tremendous help in distracting the girls while I went through the task of planning a memorial service. It was decided after several discussions with Brian's parents and his brothers that we would have a memorial service in Anchorage at the base chapel, after which he would be buried at Arlington National Cemetery. His brothers and my sister had decided to be at the memorial service in Anchorage and at the private family ceremony at Arlington. His parents had decided not to make the difficult trip to Alaska and would be meeting us all in Washington DC, along with my dad.

Many of our friends had called or sent flowers, and quite a few were willing to make the trip all the way to Anchorage for his memorial service, which really touched me. The plans for the service were coming along, and although I knew it would be difficult, I felt that it would be a fitting tribute to Brian.

None of the wives of those who died had been able to view their husbands. The crash had been so violent that all of the bodies had either been badly burned or terribly damaged. I made the decision not to have Brian's casket in the chapel during the service. It would have been more than I could bear to know that he was so close. I had already signed the papers that allowed the air force to transport his body to Andrews Air Force Base outside of Washington DC. I went for a walk by myself along the runway as the C-130 that was carrying his body taxied down the runway and took off.

As I watched the plane get smaller and smaller in the sky as it took my husband away, I felt an overwhelming sense of loss and loneliness. Not only did I miss just talking to him every day, hearing him laugh, and the little things like listening to him sing in the shower, I missed the physical part of him too. I missed his beautiful smile, his gentle hands, and the broad chest that I had laid my head on every night that we were together for the past thirteen years. I had been keenly aware since that first morning of the emotional pain and loss, but as I watched that airplane take him away from me forever, I felt the pain of the loss of the physical part of Brian for the first time. I felt like he was really truly gone from me in every sense of the word, and it hurt more than I can say.

The memorial service was the next day, and we made it through the day the best that we could. I still felt numb, but the presence of so many people who genuinely cared for and admired Brian made the reason we were there a little easier to bear. I was proud of the girls and the way they handled the enormous stress of the day. They had carefully helped me choose the pictures of their daddy that they loved the most, and we displayed them on a big board outside in the entrance of the chapel, along with a book where people could share their favorite memories of Brian. Years later, I took great comfort in reading the things that people had written about him and how he had been a positive influence in so many lives.

Much to the surprise of almost everyone, I had decided that I wanted to say a few words at the service. My mother was afraid that it would be too hard on me, but I felt strongly that it was something that I needed to do to honor Brian and to take advantage of the opportunity to speak to the many military wives I knew would be there. When it was my turn to speak, I quietly bowed my head and asked God to give me the strength to say the things I wanted to say, and I thanked him for seeing me through this far. Then I rose from my seat and walked to the pulpit. There were hundreds of people there, and as I looked out at the sea of faces before me, I was suddenly filled with a peace and calm that I hadn't experienced since Brian's beeper had gone off that night at dinner. I cleared my throat and began to speak.

"A little over thirteen years ago, a tall, handsome young captain named Brian walked into the little bookshop where I was working and changed my life forever. I didn't know the first thing about being a military wife, but I did know that I had fallen in love with an extraordinary and exceptional man. He was everything I ever could have asked for in a husband from the first moment we met until he kissed me good-bye when he left our home for the last time just a few nights ago. He was warm and funny, and he was the best friend I will ever have. He loved his girls and couldn't wait to see their smiling faces whenever he came home from a trip. They would run into his arms, and he would hug them tight and swing them around. I will always be so grateful to Brian for being the kind of father he was to our girls because he left them with nothing but happy and loving memories that I know will be a comfort to them for the rest of their lives.

"I want to take a moment to speak to the military wives who are here today. I know that this accident has taken away something from all of us. Every day we watch our husbands leave, never really knowing if or when they'll be back; it's a fact of life for most of us. And this past week, you all have seen the very worst of what being a military wife can mean. But as I stand before you now, not as a military wife but as a military widow, I hope that you will always remember that the contribution that you make is so very important. It's important not only to your children and your husband but to the command he's under and the country that he serves. I'm sure many of you are wondering if what has happened to me will happen to you, but chances are, God willing, none of you will ever know what this feels like. And even as I grieve for Brian and face the reality of life without him, I will always be proud that I was a military wife and that I was married to a man who saw the importance in honor, integrity, and service to his country. He believed in what he was doing, and when God called him home, he was doing what he loved. I know that in the difficult days ahead, that will give me comfort.

"I am so grateful for the support you all have given us during the past few days. I will miss the friendships we have enjoyed throughout Brian's career, and I will miss being a military wife. But as I leave here today, the one thing I will carry with me is how very blessed I am to have known and been loved by Brian, and I know in my heart that I will see him again someday. Until that time, the memory of all that he was to me will sustain me."

The words I spoke that day were true. My memories of Brian and our happiness as a family have seen me through many dark times when I began to feel sorry for myself and allow the futile thoughts of "why" enter my mind. I'll never know why, so I have to live each day thinking only of what I do know. And that is that I loved Brian with all my heart, and I know that he loved me and our girls. The happiness we shared in the time we had together is something many people never know in their lifetime. So I'm grateful; every single day, I'm simply grateful.

Paulette

A LIGHT IN THE DARKNESS

If someone had told me when I was a teenager that I was going to grow up and be a minister's wife, I probably wouldn't have been all that surprised, but if they had told me that I was going to be a military chaplain's wife, I probably wouldn't have believed them. Living in a small town in North Dakota, I'd never even seen anyone who was in the military, so it would have been a big stretch for me to imagine myself as a military wife. But God has a way of bringing people into your life right when you least expect it.

My grandfather had been a preacher and, as the head of our large family, had been revered and beloved by us all. He had a way of looking at a person and somehow knowing when they were troubled. He was a true believer of the phrase "the eyes are the window to the soul." More than once I had been on the receiving end of a kind but questioning stare from my grandfather, whereupon I was sure that he somehow knew about every misdeed I had committed. He knew that my older, unmarried sister was expecting a baby almost before she knew it herself, and somehow he sensed that my aunt Lillian was carrying the crushing knowledge of her terminal cancer even though she hadn't told a soul and had sworn the doctor to secrecy. He always said that shame and fear were heavy burdens to carry all by yourself, and that's why God had given us friends and family to help us make our way through life. He never judged or criticized; he was just there, kind of like a big, solid oak tree that you could lean on when you were tired or that would give you shade when you were desperate to get out of the sun. It was to this grandfather that I ran crying for comfort after the most humiliating experience of my young life.

I suppose that everyone, at some point in their lives, suffers the indignity of rejection and humiliation. Some of us are fortunate enough to suffer these experiences in private, maybe when a spouse or an intimate friend hurts us deeply by something they've said or done. Or maybe a parent criticizes, belittles, or even rejects us, and the pain is intense. But as horrible as these times may be, we can lick our wounds in private. When the embarrassment is a public thing, humiliation has an audience. It's kind of like throwing a rock into the middle of a quiet pond; the ripple effect just keeps going and going, and there is no way to bring it back. This is exactly what happened to me when I was a tender fifteen years old.

My school was having the dreaded "Sadie Hawkins" dance, where the girls were supposed to ask the boys to be their dates. Never having been on a date and knowing very little about boys, the whole idea seemed fraught with horror from start to finish. I was only half right; the horror came right at the start, and I never even got to the finish! I didn't really even want to go, but my mother was insistent. She was on the decorating committee for the dance and was going as a chaperone, and she insisted that my days of being a "wall-flower" had to come to an end. After all, that's how she had landed my dad. To her it was all very simple. She asked my dad to the dance, he said yes, they began dating and years later married, and everyone lived happily ever after. Maybe it worked for them, but not for me.

Bowing to parental pressure with the dance looming ever closer, I chose a boy I thought was kind of cute and that I thought had the least chance of rejecting me outright. I got up the nerve to ask him, but I made a huge tactical error. I asked him at school, while he was standing by his locker, with half a dozen of his friends within ear shot. I cleared my very dry throat, tried my best to look him straight in the eye, and asked Michael to the dance. As I stood there, awaiting my fate, I thought I saw his lip twitch. Then he smiled and said, "Sure."

A wave of relief washed over me, and my legs suddenly felt weak. My relief was short lived because just as I began to smile back at him, he added, "When hell freezes over!" As he and his friends burst out laughing, my legs went from weak to positively wobbly, and I prayed that they would hold out long enough for me to make a hasty exit without embarrassing myself any further. What I wanted to do was smack him, shake him, and ask him how he could be so mean, especially when it had taken me so much courage just to get up the nerve to ask him. But instead I just mumbled something semi-coherent like, "Well, okay then, thanks anyway," and bolted. All I knew was that I had to get away from that school before all the tears that were welling up behind my eyes came pouring down my face, so I ran straight for home.

Nine times out of ten, humiliation eventually turns to anger. So when I got a stitch in my side from running so hard and had to slow down, that's what happened to me. I got really, really mad. I was mad at Michael for treating me so badly, I was mad at my mother for making me ask him in the first place, and I was mad at my best friend whose date had said yes right away and had told me, "It's no big deal, Paulette; just do it" But most of all, I was mad at myself for being stupid enough to ask him in front of his friends and for not having the guts to tell him off right then and there. By the time I made it home and saw my grandfather sitting peacefully on our porch swing, whittling on a piece of wood, the hurt and humiliation pushed my anger aside, and I started crying again. My grandfather saw me coming and quickly put his knife and carving under the swing so his arms were free. I ran right into them and cried and cried. He didn't say a word; he just held me close and let me get it out of my system, knowing that I would tell him everything when I was ready, and I did. He listened, saying very little, and I found that after sharing my horrible experience with someone who loved me, I felt a little better.

I had stopped crying, and we just sat there gently swinging back and forth. I was waiting for the words of wisdom I knew would come, but as always, my grandfather thought carefully before he spoke.

"You know, Paulette, you're right. What that boy did was very unkind, and I know it hurt you deeply. But many people don't intend the pain they end up inflicting on other people. They are just thoughtless, careless, or unable to understand how they would feel if the situation were reversed. This is especially true for young teenage boys who are trying to pick their way through the landmines of boy-girl relationships. I know you were embarrassed, and I know how that must have felt. It happens to all of us at one time or another. What happened to you was out of your control, but how you respond from here is completely up to you. You can stay mad, let it eat at you, and possibly even let it make you feel bad about yourself, or you can try to let it go and chalk it up to experience. The best thing to do in my opinion is to just forgive the boy for his insensitivity and put it behind you. And someday, when you have a child of your own and their feelings get hurt or they are embarrassed like you were today, you will be able to tell them that you know exactly how it feels, and they will love you for it."

I smiled, amazed at how wise my grandfather was, how lucky I was to have him, and how much better he always made me feel. After a minute or two, he gently lifted my head off his shoulder, looked into my face, and said, "And one more thing I want you to remember: you are a wonderful, beautiful, delightful young lady, and what happened today doesn't change that one bit. I promise you that someday, you will meet someone special, and he will recognize and love you for all the wonderful things that you are. He would rather walk through fire than hurt you the way you were hurt today, okay?"

"Okay, Grandpa," I replied. Little did I know that three short years from that day as Grandpa and I sat together on that swing, he would be the reason that my "special someone" found me and that I would be forever grateful, even though that magical day would be one of the saddest of my life.

I still remember it like it was yesterday. The air was cool, and the leaves were an amazing shade of gold, with a little red and yellow mixed in. It was a beautiful fall day, and I remember thinking that it seemed like since my grandfather was now in heaven, he had asked God to give us a beautiful day to help us remember that there was still joy and happiness to be found even on the day of his funeral.

It was very warm in the church. My grandfather had known so many people throughout his life, and it seemed that every single one of them had come to pay their respects. I was glad of course that so many people remembered and cared for him, but it wasn't the same for me. He was my grandpa, and our relationship had been special and personal. He was much more than a preacher to me, and suddenly I felt alone, like no one else in that crowded room could possibly feel about him like I did. I was suddenly desperate for some cool air on my face and a reprieve from all the condolences and good wishes from people I didn't even know.

So it was that I found myself leaning against a massive tree, watching the sunlight and wind play with the leaves, sending them skipping and twirling across the ground, when I looked up and realized that someone was approaching me. He wasn't anyone that I knew, but I was immediately intrigued by his appearance. For one thing, he was wearing a military uniform, from which service I had no idea. He also had a very distinct way of walking. It was a strong, purposeful stride, and I noted that his legs were very long. As he got closer, I could see that he was handsome and clean shaven, and his hair was very neat and short with only a little patch on the top that had been displaced by the wind. I found myself straightening up and wondering about the state of my own hair since I'd been standing in the wind for at least twenty minutes.

He was suddenly there before me. I waited for some sort of introduction, but he seemed momentarily caught up in the sight of me standing there beside the tree. He told me later that he had been mesmerized by the delicate way I looked, with my long hair blowing in the wind and my face pale and sad, with my cheeks red from the cold and my eyes large and questioning with the thickest set of lashes he had ever seen. I began to feel a little strange, so I said, "Yes, can I help you?"

He shook his head and said, "Yes, I'm sorry. My name is Daniel Lockett, and you are Paulette?"

"Yes. Do I know you?"

He went on to explain that he was the grandson of one of my grandfather's closest friends from his army days. He was there at the request of his grandfather, who had wanted very much to pay his respects by attending the service but was too ill to travel, so he sent Daniel in his place with condolences for the family.

"Are you in the army too?"

He smiled and said that no, he was a chaplain in the navy. I wondered how he knew my name, but he went on to explain that through the years my grandfather had sent pictures of our family in the letters he sent. As a result, Daniel had a good idea of what I might look like, although he was quick to add that I was much prettier than he anticipated. He offered me his arm and asked if he could walk me back to the church so he could speak with my mother and my grandmother. I took his arm and walked with him, inwardly grinning that Grandpa had been right, that maybe this was my special someone, the final and most precious gift he could ever give me.

A little over a year later, I walked out of that same church on Daniel's arm as his new bride, and my life as a chaplain's wife began.

Being the wife of a minister isn't always an easy job. There seems to be a general feeling from people that you should be a good example for your husband's congregation, that you should be willing to work on every committee, teach Sunday school and Bible school, and make the costumes for the Christmas play. And heaven forbid that you should look anything less than neatly dressed and pressed, sitting in the front row staring adoringly at your husband while he speaks. Little did they know that in most cases I had already heard my husband's sermon the preceding week as he practiced. It was always interesting to me to try and guess how many of my suggestions he would end up incorporating in his sermon each Sunday. I know that it gave him strength each Sunday to see me smiling up at him.

Most times after church I would collect our children, one boy and two girls, and head home to prepare supper while my husband would greet as many people as possible and usher the stragglers out of the church. He would arrive home, always taking a little bit longer than I thought was necessary, with a tale of this person or that desperate to "have a word" with him. Although my husband was always available during the week for counseling, many times people would choose Sunday to approach him, more out of convenience, I was always certain, than real necessity. Some days of course, there were church picnics to attend, which extended our "church family" time and ate away significantly into our "home family" time.

There was a time when I was comfortable with all of this and understood the role that I was supposed to play. But then as time wore on always being on display and many times having the sole responsibility for the house and children while my husband was busy with his church began to feel like a burden. Suddenly one day, it seemed that everyone else's problems were more important to him than we were, and I began to wonder what was happening to us. As burdensome as this lifestyle can be, it was exacerbated by the fact that my husband was a military chaplain, which adds an entire other element to the equation. Not only was I expected to participate in church activities, but being a member of the officers' wives community required a great deal of my time as well. There always seemed to be a luncheon, a ceremony, a trip, or an activity that I felt I needed to be a part of, and as the chaplain's wife, it was noticed when I didn't attend.

For years I kept all of this going. When we were stationed at a base, I was there for everything I possibly could be, and if Daniel was attached to a unit afloat, then I stayed behind and did what I could to support the wives dealing with all the pressures of having a husband gone for long periods of time. I also tried to be there for our three children and cope with the normal needs and demands they placed on me. I felt for years that somehow I'd managed to keep my head above water, but one day something changed. I felt like I was going down and that this time I wasn't going to be able to get myself back up.

I woke up one morning with the thoughts of all that I had planned for the day, and before I'd even gotten out of bed, it all seemed overwhelming. In fact, I had no desire to even get out of bed. I felt tired and sad for no apparent reason and found that I could cry at the slightest little thing. After dragging myself through my early morning routine of getting the children up and out the door, instead of getting my own shower and starting my day, all I wanted to do was sit at the table and stare out the window. I didn't want any music or any sound; I just wanted to sit there and stare … at nothing. I looked into the kitchen, and even the simple task of loading the dishwasher seemed beyond me. It seemed almost as if my mind had snapped, and suddenly nothing mattered anymore.

I turned my head slowly and looked at the stack of bills that I needed to pay and get into the mail by that day or they would be late, but I didn't care. I glanced at the clock and saw that within an hour, four of my friends would arrive to take me on our weekly shopping and lunch trip that had always been a bright spot in my week. The tears began to well up in my eyes. I had no desire to go at all; it was just all too much, so I sat there. I tried to make myself breathe slowly, hoping to stem the rising tide of anxiety that was coming over me. But all I could feel was a powerful need to get back into bed and sink into the dark and silent world of sleep.

I went to the phone and called my best friend to tell her that I couldn't make the trip. I asked if she would mind taking my kids to her house after school. She agreed and was concerned, but I told her that I just had a headache and needed a day in bed. I turned off the phone, locked the door, and walked slowly back into my room. I pulled down the shades, took off my pajamas, and climbed into bed. I lay there staring at the ceiling, desperate for sleep to come, but instead what I got was a rush of hot burning tears that seemed to come from nowhere. I closed my eyes and just let them come. I felt powerless to stop them, so they continued until I cried myself to sleep. What I didn't realize at the time was that I had just taken my first step into the suffocating world of depression.

Of course I knew people who had suffered from depression. Daniel had counseled many people dealing with depression after the death of a loved one or the occurrence of some unwanted, life-changing event. I knew that even happy occasions like marriage and the birth of a child could trigger depression. But I couldn't understand why, after all this time, with no particular, overwhelming event to change my life, I felt so helpless and despondent. I realized at the end of that very long first day that I was depressed, but it didn't occur to me that this new, unwanted companion was there to stay.

I had to learn to cope with the way I was feeling or let it completely rule my life. Unfortunately, this took me a while to figure out. As the days turned into weeks then months, it became increasingly harder for me to hide my despair from Daniel and our children, and even eventually from our friends and my husband's congregation. All the things I had always done with very little effort were suddenly more than I could possibly accomplish. The normal things that people expected of me and had always depended on me for became burdens of responsibility that I could no longer bring myself to deal with.

Daniel was patient, and he tried to be understanding. He helped more around the house when he could, tried to give me more quiet time, and gave me a couple of books to read that he had recommended to others that he hoped would help. But after months of not much improvement, he too began to feel helpless and frustrated at my inability to identify what was bothering me, why the depression had such a strong grip on me. Daniel had always prided himself on what a model family we were. Our home ran like a well-oiled machine, everyone doing their part so that he could focus on his ministry. But now there was a breakdown in the system, and it was me. I knew that he loved me and the kids, I never questioned that, but I did begin to wonder about the toll this depression was taking on my marriage. I think for one of the first times in his life, he began to wonder if God was really hearing him. He prayed for me every day, but when there was no change, he began to wonder why this was happening and what we had done to deserve this. He questioned me daily about why I was so depressed, and the answer was always the same: "I have no idea." It was like he expected me to sort it all out, find out the cause, and fix it. Of course he knew it wasn't that simple, but unlike when he was counseling military personnel or their families, this was personal. He couldn't leave it at the door when he got home. It was with him all the time, and like with me, it began to feel like we were in prison. The guilt was overwhelming. I knew that I was making him miserable. I knew that I was miserable and that our children had noticed the change in the normal routine of our lives. I was desperate to make it better. It didn't take long for me to realize that when some-one in the family has a broken leg, everyone limps.

I had confided in a few close friends that I was dealing with depression, and they were sympathetic. But unless you have lived with it, you can't really understand how powerless you are to make it stop. On those occasions when we had gone to the home of a military family to help deal with the loss of family member, I was always sure that I could under-stand how they were feeling because I could recognize grief and could see the effects of it firsthand. I cringe now at the many times I said, "I know how you feel." In reality, I didn't know how they felt because it had never happened to me. I still had my husband and my children waiting for me at home, so how could I possibly really understand how these women were feeling?

I realized the error in my thinking when time and again a friend or my mother-in-law would say something like, "I just can't understand what you have to be depressed about. You have everything in the world, and that should make you happy. Why can't you just appreciate your life and snap out of it!" As if it was that easy. That's the biggest problem with depression. Someone who has never experienced it has a hard time understanding how powerful and debilitating it can be. Everyone experiences down days now and then; that's normal. But eventually it passes, you feel better, and things get back to normal. With true depression, it doesn't go away, no matter how much you want it to.

One day I tried to explain my inability to control it to friend after she suggested that soaking in a warm bubble bath with a glass of wine and some candles would make me feel better. She was probably right; it would have made me feel better, for a short time. But then that same old feeling would creep back, and I'd be right back where I started. I told her that it was like the difference between someone who suffered from the occasional headache and a person who suffers from migraines.

Most people get a headache from time to time, and they feel lousy; they take a pain reliever and maybe rest for a while, and it eventually goes away without too much disruption in their routine. For people with migraines, it's a whole different story. A simple aspirin won't do. It can become completely debilitating, with pain so severe that even the slightest bit of light or sound can be excruciating and lead to vomiting and total inability to function. So it would be very difficult for a person who suffers only occasional, mild headaches to claim they understand how it feels to be a chronic migraine sufferer. It's the same way with depression; just because you have the occasional down day doesn't mean you can understand the full meaning of chronic, debilitating depression.

Both my husband and my mother suggested after weeks turned into months that I should speak with one of the doctors on base about any medication that might help. But for a long time, I fought the idea. I was afraid that in the fishbowl confines of the base, that somehow, someone would find out that the chaplain's wife was taking anti-depressants, and it would reflect poorly on Daniel. I could hear the gossip already: "I wonder how long she's been like this?" or "How could someone who is supposed to be so spiritual be depressed?" Gossip is like a children's game of telephone gone bad. Things change with every passing from one person to the next, and before you know it, the truth becomes buried so deep inside the rumors that you can't see it at all. And I just wasn't willing to risk it, so I suffered. That was a mistake I finally realized one Sunday at church.

The children's choir was singing at the base chapel on this particular day, and it had been a frustrating one from the start. We all woke up late, I was exhausted as I so often was these days, and getting everyone ready for church seemed like a monumental task. But I knew the kids couldn't be late for practice, so somehow we made it on time, with me feeling unnecessarily stressed and burdened. As I sat there in the pew listening to the children singing, their faces happy and bright, I was mad. For no reason whatsoever, I was mad. It suddenly occurred to me that I was annoyed because everyone around me seemed happy, like they were enjoying the day, and I was jealous. I hadn't known simple, peaceful happiness for so long; I was resentful that they did. I realized later that what I was feeling on that day was irrational and a clear sign that I did not have the depression or my emotions under control, but at the time, all I knew was that I wasn't happy. So when our youngest, Blake, all of four little innocent years old, began to pick his nose in the middle of singing, I was embarrassed and furious.

Of course, your child picking at his nose in front of the church is not something to be proud of, certainly, but the "old me" would have realized that he had just been getting over a cold the week before, his nose was probably bothering him, and what he was doing wasn't the end of the world, especially since this was just a rehearsal and the chapel was only scattered with other choir parents. But the new depressed me didn't see it that way at all, and I was trying to catch his eye. When he finally saw me, I shook my head furiously *no!* But in his little four-year-old mind, he needed to explain himself, so he yelled out at the top of his lungs, echoing out across the chapel, "But, Mom, I gots boogers!"

My embarrassment was complete, and with no regard for my son's feelings, I stood up and yelled at him, "Blake Daniel Lockett, you come here right this minute!"

Suddenly a deathly quiet came over the room as my hateful screeching at my son echoed back at me across the beautiful stone walls of the chapel. I couldn't believe what I had just done. What was happening to me? I couldn't even believe it was my voice that I was hearing. I saw the other parents staring at me, and you could have heard a pin drop as my little son, eyes as big as saucers, walked slowly down the aisle to me, not at all sure what was going to happen to him once he got there, since the wild-eyed woman waiting for him didn't look anything like his mommy. I dragged him out of the church, desperate to get away from the eyes that I could feel boring holes in my back, when my husband appeared quickly at our sides and led us into a side room where we could have some privacy. I could tell that he was furious; I could see it by the firm set of his jaw. But when he scooped Blake up, his voice was as gentle as ever.

"What's the matter, buddy, your nose still bothering you?" My son nodded silently, his eyes full of tears, not sure what to expect next. My husband gently wiped Blake's nose, gave him a kiss on his forehead, and said, "I think that's better now. You were doing a great job singing. You want to go back out there and finish your practicing?" Blake gave a little nod, and my husband turned to me and said calmly, "Wait just a minute. I'll be back and we can talk."

I nodded silently as he closed the door behind them. I just sat there. My heart was pounding, but I felt deathly calm. I knew I had just embarrassed myself, my son, and my husband, but I was too tired and depressed to care. At that particular moment, sitting in a place that had always brought me comfort and peace, I really didn't even care if I lived or died. I felt as if the depression had won. I was just too tired to try and fight it anymore. I was so numb inside, I didn't even cry; there were no tears left.

When my husband returned a few minutes later, I expected him to be furious with me for the scene I had just created, but instead, he seemed sad. He sat down in front of me, took my hands, and bowed his head to pray. He asked for God's blessing on me and our children, and then he did something I didn't see coming at all. He asked forgiveness for himself for not recognizing the level of despair and agony that I had reached because of the depression. He prayed for God to open his eyes to the needs of his family and to help him to be all that God intended for him to be as a husband and a father. Then he said something that brought me back to reality. He thanked God for me and for our marriage. He thanked him for our grandfathers who had brought us together, and he thanked him for the wonderful life he knew was waiting for us. Daniel finished his prayer, kissed my hand, and told me that he loved me. I was speechless. He apologized for not having been there for me and really taking the time to see how much I was suffering. I think he finally understood that depression is like a disease and that I couldn't change it or fix it on my own. He vowed at that moment to help me find myself again and to find the happiness that I had been incapable of for so long.

It was a turning point in my battle with depression. It didn't change things overnight, but coping with any illness is easier when you have someone there who will love you in spite of whatever hardships go along with it. For me, the road to recovery started with admitting that I couldn't control the depression, and, like with many other illnesses, I would need medication. It was hard to get past the stigma of having to take an anti-depressant, but a nurse once told me that it's no different than any other disease that requires medical intervention. Would a diabetic choose not to take his insulin because he was worried about what other people thought and risk significant harm to himself?

I began to wonder why it had taken me so long to get to this point when within a month of starting the medication I was already feeling better. Six months later, I was beginning to feel like myself again, and I was able to get up each morning looking forward to the day instead of dreading it. And every morning when I took my pills, instead of being resentful that I suffered from depression, I decided to be grateful that there was something I could take that would help me control it. It wasn't a perfect cure; some days were harder than others, and it took a while to get the dosage just right. But there was no doubt that my quality of life had improved, and for that I was very appreciative and so were Daniel and the kids.

I thought back on the words my grandfather had said to me on the swing that day when I was fifteen. He told me that the pain that I was suffering through on that day would help me someday to better understand my children when something like that happened to them. Of course I hope that my children will never have to suffer through the pains of chronic depression. But I hoped that sometime, some good could come from my experience, and I would have the opportunity to help ease someone else's pain caused by depression. It was almost a year later when the phone rang in the middle of the night when I was given just such an opportunity.

A phone call in the middle of the night is seldom, if ever, good news. And so it was on that night when our phone rang and Daniel found himself listening to the sobbing of a young teenage girl who was a member of our congregation. After a moment or so, he was able to discern that the girl's mother had just been taken to the hospital by ambulance after an attempted suicide. Knowing that her father was out of the country and there were three younger children at home, we immediately made the decision to go over to their house and leave our children in the care of our next-door neighbor.

When we arrived, an ashen-faced girl answered the door, fell into my arms, and burst into tears. "How could she do this to us … how could she want to leave us?" She was clearly distraught and in need of some calm words and reassurances that everything would be okay. I asked after her younger brothers and sisters and learned that the youngest two were asleep, and her brother, just a year younger than she, was sitting in the living room talking to a neighbor who had been called over. He, too, looked pale and upset, but he had not given way to tears yet. As I led Miranda through the kitchen into the den area where her brother was sitting, I noticed a pile of bloody towels in the sink and motioned for my husband to take care of it. As he went quietly about the task of cleaning up, we joined her brother Mitch on the couch. The neighbor who had been sitting with Mitch quietly got up to go talk to Daniel.

Immediately when I sat down, the boy asked if someone had notified his dad yet that his mom was in the hospital. I answered honestly that I didn't know, but that I knew Chaplain Lockett would make sure that he was told as soon as it was possible if he hadn't already been notified. He then asked if I thought that he would come home soon, and I assured him that I thought he would be there as soon as possible. However, I wasn't sure how far away he was or how easy it would be to reach him.

We sat in a heavy silence for a moment, and then I pulled them close and told them that I knew for a fact how much their mother loved them and that I was sorry she was in so much pain that she had tried to hurt herself. They both had a lot of questions, some I could answer, some I felt I couldn't. But their primary concern was, why, if she loved them, would she have tried to kill herself and leave them alone? It was a tough question, but as I thought for a moment how to answer, I was reminded of how deep my desperation was when I was in the midst of my bout with depression. And it occurred to me just then that this might be my opportunity to use the pain that I had suffered for the good of someone else. Maybe my experience with depression could help these two children try to understand the way their mother may have been feeling. So I said a quick prayer and began to comfort them the best I could.

I started by saying, "You children are old enough to understand what depression is. Has your mother ever discussed it with you before?"

"Yes," said Mitch, "it's the thing that makes her sad all the time."

"Yes, that's true,," "but there is a little more to it than that."

Before I began to explain what depression is, I told them that I had talked to their mother on several occasions and I knew for certain that she loved them all very much. On her own, she never would have wanted to leave them, but with the disease of depression, the pain can become so intense that you feel there is no way to ever feel better.

"Sometimes people begin to think of doing things, like your mother did, that they never would have considered under normal circumstances. Being depressed is an illness like any other, and your mother is suffering the worst kind of depression you can have. But like other illnesses, it can be cured, and I am sure that your mother will get the help she needs to feel better." They thought about this for a moment, and I wasn't sure that they really understood what I had just told them. I felt I needed to add one more thing. "I want you children to know that your mom is going to be okay. I know because I had depression too."

They both looked up at me with a little bit of hope. "Did you try and do the same thing that our mother did?" Mitch asked me.

I told them that no, I had not gotten to that point, that I had decided I needed to get help from the doctor, and that he prescribed some medicine for me that helped me cope. "But there were many, many times when I felt the desperation that your mother felt tonight, and I understand how badly your mom must have felt to do this. It doesn't make her a bad person; she just needs some help right now, and we can all make sure that she gets the help she needs."

"Why didn't she ask us for help ... or Daddy?" Miranda asked quietly.

"Well, I don't know for sure," I responded, "but I do know that when you are depressed, you feel very lonely, even if there are other people all around you. You think that no one will really understand how you feel. And sometimes it's very hard for an adult to ask for help, especially from their children. Maybe this is your mom's way of asking for help, and now we know how we can help her. The doctors will talk to her, and they will help her with her depression. She will be okay. It might take a while, but she will be okay. Just remember that, okay?"

Just then Daniel walked in and told us that he had talked to the hospital and that their mother was resting and was going to be okay. Both children began to cry when they heard this, and Daniel and I put our arms around them and started to pray with them. When we were through, we told them that we would be with them until their grandfather could get there and that their dad was in the process of being notified and would be there as soon as he could. They asked what they should tell their younger brother and sister, and we said that until their dad got home and decided exactly what he wanted to tell them, the best thing was probably to say that Mommy is sick and in the hospital. We all agreed that for now, that was all they needed to know.

For a moment we were all quiet, and then Mitch asked Daniel a question. "When Mrs. Lockett was sick with her depression, were you afraid?"

Daniel smiled a little, took my hand, and said, "Yes, I was afraid. She was hurting very badly, and it was hard for me to know exactly how to help her. It's always hard to see someone that you love be in pain."

Mitch looked over at me and said, "But she's all better now… right?"

Daniel smiled and said, "Yes, she is, and your mom will be too. You guys can pray for her every day, and that will help her too."

They were concerned that their dad would be mad that he had to come home before he was supposed to, and we assured them that he wouldn't be mad. When something like this happens and the sailor or soldier needs to come home, everyone understands.

"I'm sure that your dad wants to be home right now to be with your mom and to look after you guys," I said.

"I don't know… I think that he is pretty far away. Who is going to take care of us until he gets home?" Miranda asked.

We gently reminded them that their grandfather was coming and was anxious to help take care of them and that there were lots of people from the base and the chapel that would be there to help with meals, errands, and anything else that they might need while their mother was getting better.

"I'm glad that Grandpa is coming … things always seem better when he is around," Miranda said.

Mitch nodded and agreed. "Yeah, we'll be okay if Grandpa is here … he's pretty neat."

"Really?" I said. "Because I had a grandfather that was pretty neat, and he had a way of always making me feel better, too, so I know what you mean."

Later that evening, after their grandfather arrived and had a brief chat with Daniel, we felt comfortable leaving them for a while. They were right; he did seem like a neat grandfather. In fact, he reminded me a lot of my own. Daniel and I knew as we walked slowly home through the cool air and quiet of the base that there were other issues with this family that would have to be worked out, that many times there are things that trigger the kind of depression that leads to a desperate act like this. Things like extreme loneliness from the long deployments, the temptations of infidelity that are so common among military couples, or even just the overwhelming frustration and fatigue that can result from having the sole responsibility for children and finances can become the catalyst for severe depression.

"You did a great job with those kids tonight," Daniel said as he put his arm around me. "I'm glad you felt you could share a little of your own struggles with them, just to help them see the light at the end of the tunnel … they were pretty scared."

"Yes, they were, and I remember a time when I was too. I wondered how any good could ever come of a situation as bad as my bout with depression. But thank God you were there for me, and thank God that my grandfather was there for me all those years ago."

"What do you mean exactly?"

"Long ago, when I was a child and had my feelings hurt,

my grandfather told me that whatever pain we feel in this life can be turned into something good, and he was right. Maybe, just maybe, the pain I endured with my depression was worth it, if it helps me to help someone else like Miranda and Mitch."

Then Daniel smiled and shared something with me that he never had before. He told me that on the day his grandfather had asked him to attend my grandfather's funeral in his place, he had had to break a date with a girl he had been looking forward to taking out.

I turned and looked at him in surprise. "You never told me that!"

"Oh, I didn't? It must have slipped my mind until now," he said with a grin. "Anyway, my grandfather said to me, 'Daniel, go to this funeral and pay respects for me. I have a feeling you won't be sorry that you did,' and he was right."

"And … have you ever been sorry that you came on that day?" I asked him.

"Not for a minute," he smiled. "And how about you, Mrs. Lockett? I know it's not easy being a chaplain's wife; are you ever sorry that I saw you standing by that big ole tree that day?"

As I turned to look at him in the moonlight, all the years filled with happiness, frustrations, loneliness, pride, and depression went through my mind, and I was able to look him in the eyes and tell him honestly, "Not for a minute."

Julianna
FOOD, MY NEW BEST FRIEND

I lay there in the darkness with a sick feeling in the pit of my stomach. I was alone, waiting for the alarm to go off. For months I had been marking off the days one by one on my calendar in the kitchen, waiting for the day my husband would come home from this last deployment. He had been gone for almost eight months—eight long, lonely months. Part of me couldn't wait to see him, and the other part dreaded the moment he would lay eyes on me. I had changed so much. Inside I still felt like me, but on the outside I didn't look like me. I was afraid of what my husband would say, how he would feel when he saw me.

I had seen the way a lot of the women behaved when their husbands were gone on long deployments. Some seem to handle it better than others, or maybe it just appeared that way. There were a few that always seemed to have it all together. They worked, or they were active with their children…joined clubs or volunteered. They filled their time with something, anything, to make the days go faster until their husbands would come home again.

But for others, their pastimes weren't as innocent. I knew of at least six of the ship wives who were having affairs, and I'm sure there were others who were more discreet. I heard about some who got together for boozy lunches and mindless chit chat ... anything to ease the loneliness. I knew how they felt, and there were days when I too felt the desperation that comes with long separations. The difference was that I didn't drink, take drugs, or fool around behind my husband's back. But I also didn't do anything productive, like joining a club or volunteering at a hospital.

How did I spend my lonely days? I ate. I ate and ate ... all day long, all night long. I ate when I was sad, happy, and angry; it didn't matter. In the eight months since my husband had been gone, I had found a new best friend ... food. It was perfect! It was always there when I needed it; I wasn't being unfaithful to my husband but could enjoy myself just the same. I could eat alone or with friends; it didn't matter. I couldn't control much else in my life, but I could eat what I wanted when I wanted. It felt great. That is, until I looked in the mirror. I mean really looked in the mirror.

At first it was subtle changes. My clothes got a little tighter, my face looked a little fuller, but nothing too drastic, or so I told myself at the time. So what if I gained a little weight? Matt had gone off and left me alone for eight long months, with nothing to do but eat. And why shouldn't I? It made me happy and calmed my nerves. It gave me something to look forward to, and it was fun. The only decision I had to make in the mornings was whether I should have pancakes and sausage or eggs and bacon.

Not long after I had finished breakfast, I was already thinking about lunch. When I would go out with friends, whatever we did always involved food in some way. I felt proud that I wasn't falling into the temptation to drink too much; in fact, more than once I had been the designated driver on a night out with the girls since they all knew that I didn't drink. No, it just wasn't the same thing. Eating too much wasn't anything like drinking too much. I mean, who was I hurting? I never made a fool of myself, never said things that I regretted the next day, and never felt out of control. I was safe in the knowledge that I wasn't going to do anything to embarrass my husband. And so I lived my life doing just what I pleased. Weekends were the best. I would have a girlfriend or two over; we would get a couple of videos and order pizza. They would drink wine, and I would down two or three sodas. We always ended our evenings around the cheesecake.

Except for the fact that my husband was an ocean away, life was good and I was coping ... or was I? I hadn't always been like this. In fact, I had always taken pride in my trim, size six figure and had never had to do much to maintain it. The way I looked had always been important to Matt. In fact, on more than one occasion, he had made me feel like a "trophy wife," always wanting me to look a certain way, wearing skintight clothes that I felt drew too much attention to my figure. Matt was handsome and more than a little vain, and there were days when I wondered if my husband appreciated me for anything other than how I looked.

My first indication that something might not be right was when my sister, Justina, came to visit me. She was always so supportive and tried to make the six-hour drive to see me at least every other month each time Matt was out to sea. I had not seen her in several months. Apparently my good times with my "friend" had gotten a little out of hand because the minute she got out of the car, I could see a look of surprise on her face. I wondered if I had forgotten to comb my hair or something. I couldn't imagine why she was looking at me like that.

"My word, Jules ... you've gained so much weight!" She

and I had always been very close; we are only a year apart in age and had never beaten around the bush when it came to telling each other exactly how we felt about things, whether it was our choice of hairstyle, clothing, boyfriends, whatever. But still, her comment took me by surprise, and I was a little hurt.

"What do you mean?" "It's not that bad, is it?"

She could see the hurt look on my face and tried to rephrase her initial comment by telling me that of course it wasn't "bad." It was just that she had never seen me with this much weight on me before. We got past the awkward moment and fell into a hug, and then we got her bag and headed into the house. I asked her if she wanted to sleep with me, like we had done all our lives starting when we were toddlers, or if she wanted to stay in the little twin bed I had set up in the room that was to become a nursery someday when Matt and I started our family. She said that of course she would sleep with me, so we could talk long into the night like we always had. I told her that I had been working on dinner all day and that as soon as she wanted to, we would eat.

Justina rested for a while, and I did the finishing touches on dinner. I had fixed homemade chicken and noodles, mashed potatoes, green beans, fresh bread, and an apple pie for dessert. When I called my sister down to eat and she saw all that I had fixed, she said, "Is someone else joining us?"

"No, why?"

"Because there is enough food here for a small army!" I put my hands on my apparently much wider hips in exasperation and asked her if we were going to discuss food all weekend. What had she become all of a sudden … the food police? We sat down and quickly fell into comfortable conversation, catching up on all the family gossip. I ate like I always did and didn't think a thing of it, but when we were washing up the dishes, Justina asked me if I was pregnant. I looked at her in disbelief.

"My husband has been gone for six months; other than an immaculate conception, what are you implying?"

She was quick to say, "Nothing like that of course. But honestly, Julianna, I've been your sister for twenty-seven years, and I have never seen you eat like this before. You ate twice the amount I did for dinner. Didn't you notice that? And you have always been so slim. Is something wrong? Why have you gained all this weight?"

I just stood there, not knowing what to say. I'm not one of those people who gazes into the mirror all the time, and I hadn't really taken a good, long look at myself for a while. "I don't know; I don't think anything is wrong... Of course, I miss Matt. Now that he is assigned to this aircraft carrier, he said I can expect deployments to be anywhere from six months to a year, and they have already been delayed returning home twice. Maybe I'm not taking it as well as I thought I would." I had been wearing a lot of loose, comfortable clothing lately; maybe I had changed and just hadn't noticed.

We finished up with the dishes and watched a little TV, but we were both tired and decided to turn in early. We lay in the bed like we had done for so many years and talked for over an hour, even though we were both getting sleepy.

"Julianna, I don't want you to be mad at me for questioning you about your weight. We all love you, and we know how hard your life is with Matt away so much of the time. I hear women in my garden club complaining because their husbands play golf every Saturday morning, and they're tired of it. I feel like telling them, 'My sister hasn't seen her husband in almost eight months; you should be grateful that you have them around every weeknight and on the weekends when they aren't playing golf!' But no one really understands."

Then Justina told me that she was behind a car with a

bumper sticker that said, "Support Our Troops." When the car parked beside her in the parking lot and a woman got out, Justina asked her if she had someone close to her in the military. The lady answered no, that she just thought that people should support the troops. At that point, Justina was curious about what this woman's idea was of what it meant to "support the troops," so she asked her. She said that the woman seemed flustered and that she didn't really know what she could do; she just wanted people to know how she felt.

Justina continued on, "I told her that my brother-in-law was deployed on an aircraft carrier in the Pacific for up to a year at a time, and one good way to support the troops would be to find a way to help the families left behind."

I told Justina that I really appreciated the thought, and I knew that some of the families really struggled when their husbands were deployed. I had always been able to manage the house and our finances without any trouble, but lately, especially after the disappointment of two back to back postponements of their arrival date home, I was beginning to feel the strain. Maybe I had been turning to food and was eating a lot more than usual. I began to worry though, and early the next morning I decided to see exactly how much I had gained. I was shocked to see that it was just over twenty-five pounds. It was much more than I expected, and I wasn't happy about it, but when it came down to it, it really wasn't anyone's business but my own.

I soon realized that was not the case when the day after Justina returned home, my mother called to arrange a visit. She didn't say anything about my weight, but I knew that was why she wanted to come out to see me. Justina must have been more concerned than she let on to me. "Of course you are welcome to visit, Mom; you know that. But please don't come out here just to see how much weight I have gained. Justina is making too much out of this!"

Naturally my mother denied that was the reason and even pretended to be insulted. But I know my mother and my sister, both of whom have been thin and trim all their lives, and I knew my mother wouldn't be happy that I had "let myself go." Although I'm sure she meant to be helpful and supportive, just worrying about her coming and what she would say caused me to gain another five pounds in the two short weeks before she arrived. I was becoming obsessed with the scale in our bathroom as I watched my weight slowly creep up and up. By the time my mother arrived, I was up two sizes, from a six to a ten, and had no doubt that if I kept this up I would eventually have to buy a size twelve just to feel comfortable.

I managed to eat small amounts when my mother was there, mainly because she was watching me and insisted on making all our food while she was visiting. Her diet consisted of all the right things: fiber, fruit, vegetables, lean meats, black coffee, and diet soda, both of which I hated. I had always enjoyed my visits with my mother. We generally would laugh and have a good time shopping, talking, and sewing, just whatever. But this time I found myself anxious for her to leave so that I could be alone in the peace and quiet and I could eat what I wanted to without being watched.

Finally on her last night with me, she brought up her concern about my weight gain, which she guessed correctly was about thirty pounds and three dress sizes. It was the elephant in the living room that we had been tiptoeing around all week. She made a point of telling me how lucky I was to have Matt and that I didn't want to do anything that might jeopardize my marriage. I was furious. "Let me get this straight...Matt chooses a career in the navy *after* we are already married, that he knows will leave me alone for months on end, and I should be worried about jeopardizing the marriage just because I have gained some weight?"

My mother could tell that I was hurt and defensive, but she still felt compelled to tell me that some men just won't stand for a fat wife. I couldn't believe my ears. I know that she and Dad were a little old fashioned and that she waited on him hand and foot, but I refused to believe that my father ever would have left my mother just because she gained some weight. The whole conversation was beyond belief. She then went on to tell me that my father had not been happy when she had gained weight during her pregnancies with me and Justina and that she had had to constantly reassure him that she would lose the weight after we were born. I couldn't believe my father felt that way. I guess since none of the three of us, my mother, Justina, or I, had ever been overweight before, it just never came up. But it left me seeing my father in a whole new light and wondering if maybe Matt was going to be just like him. Somehow I already knew the answer.

Then she asked me, "Don't you ever plan on having children?"

"I'd love to," I snapped, "if Matt was ever here long enough to do something about it!"

"Well, then you don't want to start off heavy, or it will be just that much harder to lose it afterwards."

Mercifully, the discussion finally came to an end. When I took her to the airport in the morning, I was glad to see her go. *Why* was everyone making such a big deal about this? Was I not the same person I have always been? Do they think that my relationship with my husband is so shallow that it can't withstand me gaining some weight?

And that was the exact question that I was asking myself on that morning, lying there waiting for the alarm to go off. I was going to see Matt for the first time in almost eight months, and I had to admit that I did look very different than I had when he left all those months ago. But would it matter? If he really loved me, how could it? All these thoughts were churning in my head when the alarm did finally go off, and I got up to get in the shower. I had just been out to buy new clothes (which was a hard dose of reality) and had my nails done and my hair lightened, anything to help take the attention off my size.

I was nervous and excited. Whenever a ship as big as an aircraft carrier, which can hold over 6000 men, came into port, it was a beautiful sight to see. The ship would be shined up looking its best, and the men and women on board would be standing in ranks along the entire perimeter of the deck. Husbands, wives, and children would be clustered in the thousands, anxious, excited, and proud as they watched the massive ship dock with our beautiful flag flapping in the breeze. Rain or shine, hot or cold, the weather never mattered. These women and children always came and waited, nervous, happy, excited, or afraid, no matter how long it took, to watch their husbands come home.

I was amazed every time at the sheer power and glory that the ship projected as it came slowly in and how it must have made an indelible image on the minds of all the children there, bursting with the anticipation of that first hug. I had witnessed it time and again, and it never failed to move me when I saw these children, some just old enough to walk, all the way up to teenagers who for the moment weren't worried if it looked "cool" or not to be seen hugging their dad. And I was always sure that the men, even though they were tall and proud, looking straight ahead, were just as excited as their families were.

But on this particular day, I was a little worried and for the moment was glad that I hadn't found any of the wives that I knew among the masses. I just wanted to move slowly through the crowds, taking it all in and enjoying this moment in time that was bringing happiness to so many people. For right now, all the hardships, the loneliness, and the frustrations that had been endured for the last eight months were forgotten. The more seasoned wives knew too that there would be a time of transition as husbands, wives, and children learned how to function together as a family again now that Dad was back. But this moment was purely and simply about the joy and excitement of being reunited with someone that you had missed for so long. There were tears on many a face as our men and women began to slowly file down the gangway, anxiously searching the crowds for the faces of their loved ones.

It was about forty-five minutes before I finally saw Matt making his way down, and it felt like my heart skipped a beat. I tried to push to the front of the crowd of people who were talking, laughing, hugging, and crying, until I was in a position where I knew he could see me. I held my breath and waited. *Please God, don't let him be too disappointed when he sees me*, I prayed silently. Suddenly I wished that I had not been so dependent on my new friend, but I pushed it from my mind and convinced myself that it wouldn't matter. But when Matt finally picked me out of the crowd, I saw him do a double take then look more closely to be sure it was me, and in those moments, I knew that it did matter. He recovered his shocked expression and moved to hug me. He didn't say a word; he just hugged me quickly while I tried to swallow the huge lump in my throat. There was no way I could do it, though, and as the tears started to flow, I heard myself saying, "I'm sorry; I'm sorry." Matt pulled back and asked me if I was okay, and I told him that I was, but it had been a long and difficult separation for me.

The he said, "Well, I'm home now, and we can talk all about that later." As I clung to his hand, we fought our way back to the car. I noticed all the beautiful, thin wives in the clutch of their proud husbands, and I wondered for the first time in my married life if maybe Matt was ashamed of me and the way I looked. Granted, not every wife was thin, and not all were beautiful. But I had never really noticed before. I was always just comfortable in my own skin, happy with my looks, and not worried about anyone else. But now, I could feel myself comparing the way I looked to all the other wives. And again for the first time ever, I felt like I couldn't compare. I was fat now, and I felt ugly and ashamed. Then only a few seconds later, I felt mad at myself for even having those thoughts and allowing it to matter. What was wrong with me? I knew I was overwhelmed with emotion that Matt was finally home, but at the same time, I felt like I wanted to crawl into a corner and cry. I just wanted to get home, be with Matt, and have him tell me that everything was okay, that he still loved me, and that nothing, not even all the weight I had gained, could change that. But I also knew that we had some serious talking to do in the next few days. We were about to shine a light on our relationship, and I was afraid that I wouldn't like what I saw there.

Whenever a service member returns home after a long absence, there is always a period of adjustment for everyone concerned. The wives who have had to carry on without their husbands, managing the children, the finances, car repairs, homework, school conferences, the kid's sporting events, ballet, piano lessons, and taking the dog to the vet, suddenly have to fit another adult in to the routine. For the guys coming home, they have to pick their way through the tangled emotions and routines of a family that has grown and changed in their absence. Suddenly, a quick run through the drive-thru of McDonald's isn't what the husband has in mind for dinner. He thinks his son's hair is too long, his daughter's skirts are too short and her makeup too heavy, and the wife begins to ask herself how everything worked so well before he got home.

Some couples find this period of readjustment more difficult than others. For Matt and me the problems began the minute we got home and he had a chance to walk around the house and note all the changes I had made while he was away. Some he liked; others he didn't. He was less than pleased that I had rearranged all his tools in the garage and was not happy with the time, effort, and money I had invested in a nursery when we weren't even expecting yet. But he was pleased that I had managed to keep the lawn looking so good and our checkbook balanced. He was tired and edgy, a little more than usual, I thought, and was not nearly as romantic and amorous as he usually was when he arrived home after a long deployment. In fact, he hadn't even made his way into our bedroom, which before was always our first stop.

I wondered immediately if it was because of the difference in my appearance. Maybe he was just tired and stressed; it had been a long, hard tour for him too. I tried not to read anything into his current state of mind and asked him if he was hungry. He said he was, and I disappeared into the kitchen while he made his way into the bathroom to take a shower. Dinner was nice; I lit some candles and had set a beautiful table. Just for a moment I was glad that I didn't have to share him with any children.

We attempted to catch up on the little things that happened to each of us over the last months, things that weren't important enough to mention during a phone call or in a letter but nonetheless made up the fabric of our everyday lives when we were apart. Matt was happy with his new job as the head machinist in the engine room and felt like he had learned a lot on this last tour. He liked the people he worked with and had some ideas about ways he wanted to improve things when he returned to the ship. It hurt my feelings a little that he hadn't even been home for twenty-four hours and was already talking about when he went back. I pushed the thought aside and told him what little there was to tell about my time spent waiting for him to return home. In fact, as I described what I had been doing, it suddenly didn't sound like much at all, and I began to ask myself, what *had*

I been doing all this time. I mean, what did I have to show for his time away other than all this weight I had gained? Then, during dessert, he looked at me with an expression that I couldn't quite read and asked me why I had gained so much weight. I was alternately embarrassed and angry, and I wasn't sure exactly how to respond.

"I'm not exactly sure … does it matter that much to you?"

"No, I guess not. You've always had a slim figure, and I have never seen you like this before. I just wondered what happened."

The next few days were spent relatively quietly, adjusting to one another's habits and routines again. I waited several days before I brought up the subject of children, knowing that it would probably bring on some hostility between us. But after this last, long tour, I was more convinced than ever that now was the time for us to start our family. I couldn't take these long deployments by myself anymore, plus, I wasn't getting any younger. So when I thought the time was right, I brought the subject up, and as I suspected, he was less than enthusiastic.

"I just can't understand why you are so against this, Matt. You knew when you married me that I wanted children, and back then you agreed. Why have you changed your attitude so drastically?"

He said he didn't know why, but that he just wasn't ready for the responsibility of kids. He didn't think we could afford them, and he reminded me that his "old man" was never around and that he didn't want to do the same thing to a kid of his. I hastened to assure him that I would be around for our children and that he would be too when he was home.

As he sat on the couch drinking a beer, his fourth of the evening, he glanced at me and said, "From the looks of it, you had a hard time managing yourself while I was gone, let alone looking after a kid!"

I couldn't believe he had just said that.

"What in the world is that supposed to mean?"

Now we had finally gotten around to it … my weight.

"Just look at you, Julianna … you're a mess. I never thought I would see you like this. You were always so thin, and look at you now!" he said as he took another swallow of beer, searching for the courage to utter those hateful words to me. As the tears sprang to my eyes, I wanted to slap him and clenched my fists to keep from doing so.

"How dare you speak to me like that! I have been here alone for eight months, fending for myself, lonely and miserable, and you have the nerve to berate me because I have gained some weight?"

He responded hatefully by saying, "*Some* weight?"

I glared at him, not knowing what to do. I always knew he was obsessed with my appearance, but he had never been mean or cruel like this before, and I began to wonder if there was something else bothering him. I refused to believe that he could be this cold and unfeeling just because my appearance had changed. I felt like I was talking to a stranger. I asked him if he would rather I drink myself into stupor every evening or spend my lonely nights in the company of someone who didn't care about my size, and he just glared at me and said more quietly than I expected, "I don't know what I want, but coming home to a fat wife isn't it." He threw the rest of his beer away in the trashcan, stomped off to our room, and slammed the door.

The tears flowed freely now, and I felt my anger give way to embarrassment as the heat crept up my neck and into my face. Was that really all I was to him, a showpiece or some kind of trophy? I had not seen this coming, or at least that's what I told myself. Maybe on some deeper level, I knew this was where we were headed. In those moments, I felt a rush of emotion. I was angry at his reaction and cruel words, I was mad at myself for getting fat, and I was afraid that I was going to lose him. But if my gaining weight could really affect his love for me, then did we ever really have anything to begin with? If I ever became sick or disfigured in some way, would he react this way then too? Everything I thought I knew about my husband was being tossed out the window, just like when my mother told me how my father felt about her staying thin. It seemed beyond unreasonable to me that their love for us could be so intertwined with the way we look. I chose to sleep in the twin bed in our "nursery" that night, feeling closer to the idea of the child who might one day sleep there than to my own husband.

The following day, we attended a ship family picnic, and I was embarrassed to find after we arrived that everyone had been told to bring their bathing suits for a number of fun, water-type games. Even the wives joined in, and since Matt had not mentioned to me that I needed to bring my suit, I sat on the sidelines, alone and sick at the thought that my husband had intentionally neglected to tell me about the water games because he didn't want me to be seen in a bathing suit. As I sat there with a forced smile on my face, I felt hurt and neglected as my husband joined in the fun while I sat there hating him for making me feel so ashamed about my appearance. I had seen other wives on the base that were much heavier than I was, so why was I being made to feel like a criminal or an outcast? When it was time to eat, he went over to the food table, laughing and talking, totally oblivious to my discomfort. I wondered then if this was just a bump in the road of our marriage or if it was the beginning of the end.

The following weekend, Matt invited a couple over for a BBQ, and as I stood in front of the mirror, trying to find something to wear that I would feel good in, a very attractive woman wearing a short sun dress and cute strappy sandals arrived with her husband and two bottles of wine. As I watched my husband greet her with an enthusiastic hug, I wondered how well he actually knew her and what kind of afternoon this was going to be. As the day progressed and we chatted, snacked, and got to know each other, I had the gnawing feeling that my husband and this woman knew each other better than I realized. I had never seen Matt be overly flirtatious before, and as I observed her husband, it didn't seem that he was particularly concerned by their attention to one another. I began to tell myself that I was just imagining it and that the current state of unrest in our marriage was causing me to be paranoid, but after a closer look I realized she was just his type … beautiful, flashy, and dressed to kill. The day ended pleasantly, and I put the thought from my mind, for a while at least.

Then a few days later, when I was babysitting the children of one of my best friends in her home on the other side of the base, I saw them. At first I wasn't sure it was Matt; he said that he had meetings all day and would be home late. But as I was outside with the children, pushing them on the swings, I heard my husband's laugh, deep and unmistakable, and I began to look around at the many windows of the houses that backed up to the community playground. It didn't take me long to find him; I would know that profile anywhere. I had not told him that I would be babysitting over there that day, or I'm sure he would have been more cautious. But he thought that I was home, working on a scrapbook that I was doing as a birthday gift for Justina.

As I stood there, watching them, Matt wearing the shirt I had just given him days earlier and that I had commented that he looked so handsome in, I felt my mouth go dry and my stomach roll. This couldn't be. Yet in that instant, I knew that it was and that my marriage was over. I felt myself break out in a cold sweat and turned away from the scene, having witnessed more than enough to know that this was not the man I had married, the man I thought I knew, that I loved. The man I thought I knew never would have done this to me, and I felt like a fool … a stupid fool. I was nothing more than a statistic. Another military wife who foolishly thinks that "her" husband would never cheat, that "her" husband is different. I realized that I wasn't any better or different than any of those wives that I had heard about and felt sorry for. I wasn't immune to the strain that long separations can take on a relationship. I wasn't immune to the loneliness that consumes you when your husband is so far away and you're living every day just waiting for his return. And I certainly wasn't immune to the temptation to fill that hole in my life with something like food. In the painful days and weeks that followed, as Matt tried to justify his infidelity or blame it on me, I realized that we had both been searching for a way to fill the emptiness. I coped by longing for children to fill the void and using food to soothe the pain. Matt coped by looking outside his marriage for the confirmation he needed to make himself feel like a man. Apparently the affair had been going on for a long time, and my weight gain just gave him the excuse he needed to put me aside. When push came to shove and he returned home, but not to the ideal wife he thought he left behind, he couldn't handle it. He just wasn't able to see past it, and in some ways, he felt like having a fat wife was a negative reflection on him and made him less of man. So he left, and I didn't try to stop him.

It had all gone so wrong, so suddenly, that for the first few months, I was in shock. I didn't want him back because somewhere deep inside, I knew that it wasn't me. At first I blamed myself, thinking that if I hadn't gained the weight, he never would have left. Then I realized that if that was all it took to shake our relationship to its core, we must not have had much of a foundation to begin with. I knew plenty of couples who loved and supported each other through much more life-shattering events than a thirty-pound weight gain, and their marriages were still strong. In time I was able to see that our relationship was weak from the start and that maybe, somewhere deep inside, I knew it. I wanted to build a life and a family, and Matt just wanted to have fun and come home to a perfect Barbie wife who looked good on his arm. I learned too late that he didn't want the complications of a deep and meaningful relationship. He was more comfortable with his emotions just skimming the surface.

Do I miss Matt? Yes, there are days when I think about the good times that we shared and the joy and pride I felt being a military wife. I miss the camaraderie among the other wives, the instant friendships, and the excitement of never knowing where you would move to next. But I don't miss those feelings of doubt and insecurity that were a part of my marriage to Matt. I don't miss the way he made me feel about myself when he was unable to accept me for who I was and see beyond the external into all that I am as a woman and a person. And although I am almost thirty-one years old now and not yet a mother, I am grateful that we never had children. It would have been too hard on our children to try to live up to their father's expectations of the way they should be rather than being accepted for who they are. And who knows … maybe someday soon I will have a chance to be a mother and a military wife again.

I've lost some of the thirty pounds, but not all of it; however, I am happy with myself and who I have become in the past two years since Matt and I divorced. Now I spend my time helping young military wives learn new ways of coping with the ever-demanding challenges of being a military wife. I help them learn to appreciate all that they are and all they can become, which in turn helps them to become better, more confident wives and mothers. I'm proud of the work I do, and I'm proud of myself and the fact that I am making a difference in the lives of military wives, no matter how small. I'm proud too of the relationship I have with another military man who loves me, respects me, and appreciates all of me, both the inside and the out. And if anyone ever stops to ask me about what the "Support Our Troops" bumper sticker on the back of my car means to me, I'll know just what to tell them.

Paige
MEXICO, HERE WE COME!

One of the first things that an officer's wife in the United States military learns is that there are two common phrases that, when uttered by her husband, will change the course of her life. The first one is "Honey, the list is out," and the second is "Honey, the detailer called."

Let's talk about "the list" first. Every year officers have what is called an OER, or an officer evaluation report. This is an opportunity for the service member's jobs, activities, awards, and accomplishments to be recorded and reviewed by various people up the chain of command. Officers are then given marks, which indicate their various levels of competency. These OERs are compiled, and when it is time for the officer's year group to be reviewed, the documentation is ready. This is a time when a husband becomes very tense, as he knows that his promotion to the next rank depends on the promotion board's review of his record in comparison to everyone else in his group. Many times this is also accompanied by the wife asking every time her husband comes home from work, "Is the list out?" knowing full well that he would have called with the news if he had heard. But the compulsion to ask, just in case he forgot to inform her, is overwhelming.

This is compounded by the other people at work asking him if the list is out since they want to know who has been promoted and who has been "passed over," but aren't up for selection this time around and consequently aren't walking around with what feels like a bag of Mexican jumping beans in their gut. In the civilian world, it would be the equivalent of, say, eight guys knowing they are being considered as one of three who will become department heads or vice presidents in a company they have worked hard for, for many years. For those who are promoted, it means a higher rank, better pay and privilege, more responsibility, and the knowledge of being one step closer to the coveted rank of general or admiral. (Less than 1 percent of officers that start out as ensigns and first lieutenants make it all the way to flag rank.)

Next is "Honey, the detailer called." Believe me when I tell you that this phrase alone has made grown women cry. The detailer is the person responsible for deciding what your husband's next job is going to be and where on the four corners of the planet it will send him and, of course, you and any number of your children that do not want to move again. This is unless your husband has been given the "opportunity" to go to some remote location unaccompanied. Depending on how many years you have been married and how many screaming children you have at home, this can either be great news (for him) or a death sentence (for you).

This brings us to the story of how a lovely day folding laundry turned into a "Honey, the detailer called" nightmare. My name is Paige Sanders, and my husband is Zack—let me set the stage for you. We have been married for ten years, and in that time we have moved six times. We have eight-year-old twins, Seth and Cody, and my husband is a pilot in the coast guard. Now you would think that with a husband in the *coast* guard, you wouldn't have to worry about moving to a place with *no* coast. Wrong. This would explain my absolute shock and surprise (hysteria?) on the day my husband walked in the door and said with a slightly glazed look in his eyes, "Well, the detailer finally called."

"And?" I said, expecting to hear that we were headed to another flying job in Hawaii, which is what we had been told up to this point.

"Well..." he said with a pained expression on his face.

"Oh no," I sat back in my chair with a mound of laundry waiting at my feet. "Just tell me... Timbuktu... Siberia... what... ?" (I was joking.)

So I was *not* prepared when my husband said, "How about Mexico City, Mexico?" (I thought *he* was joking.)

"Right, come on, really... Where are we going?"

He proceeded to say, "No really, they asked me to be the coast guard attaché at the American embassy in Mexico City, Mexico."

"*What? What* are you saying? You mean Mexico, Mexico... the foreign country where they speak Spanish... Mexico?"

"Yep, that's the one... pretty cool, huh?" he said hopefully.

"But we don't speak Spanish, remember?"

"Well, we can learn, can't we?"

"No... we can't learn. The boys just learned how to speak English, and now we are going to tell them they have to learn to speak Spanish?"

"Paige," my husband said calmly, "the boys are eight years old and have been speaking English their entire lives... they didn't just learn. Now is the perfect time for them to learn a foreign language—"

"Okay, forget them. What about me?" I cried. "How will

we manage in a country where we can't understand what anyone is saying?"

At that point, all I could see was my image of sipping a Mai Tai on a beach in Hawaii being replaced with one of me haggling over the price of a dead chicken in the window with a guy that doesn't understand a word I'm saying.

As the shock wore off and the next few days wore on … and on … I realized we really were headed to Mexico City, one of the biggest, most crowded, most polluted cities in the world. I put a brave face on for the boys and then found out we would be living in the DC area for a year, where Zack would receive training on how to become an attaché, and we would both be sent to a foreign language school to learn Spanish. (Me back to school?)

A very real part of being a military wife is the knowledge that you will most likely move more times than you ever thought possible. And a majority of those moves will require that you sell your house. Just as a house really starts to feel like a home and you've got everything the way you want it, your husband will get orders again, and you have to leave it behind. Some wives handle this process very well; others don't. I did not, and this move to Mexico was no exception. I loved this house. We had been here for almost four years, and quite simply, I wasn't ready to leave it. More than once I found myself envying wives whose husbands' jobs didn't require constant moving and upheaval.

When we put the house up for sale, I tried not to be insulted every time someone walked into our home that I had lovingly decorated and didn't immediately fall in love with it. The appearance, cleanliness, and decorating all comes under the scrutiny of strangers as they tromp through each room making comments about this or that. My husband tried not to laugh every time I got mad after the house was shown and we didn't immediately get an offer. After six weeks and still no luck, I was a wreck. I was becoming obsessed with keeping the house clean and was constantly barking at Zack and the boys, "Pick up that towel. Don't put smudges on mirrors," and so on.

I realized that maybe I had carried things a little too far when in the middle of the night, Cody appeared at our bedside and whispered to me, "Mom, I'm just going to go into the kitchen and get some water."

"That's fine, honey. You don't have to tell me; you can just go."

He responded by saying, "I just wanted to make sure you wouldn't go in and make my bed while I was in the kitchen!"

I knew that beside me Zack was suppressing the urge to laugh, and after Cody left, I said, "Good grief… have I really been that bad?"

"Afraid so, honey," he said with a grin.

I smiled back and agreed to stop worrying about selling the house and to let everybody actually *live* in it before we moved. Less than a week later, on an especially hectic day when there were dishes in the sink, towels on the floor in the bathroom, and the boys' beds weren't made, someone came through and we sold it. I just should have left it a mess; we would have sold it months earlier. Who knew?

The next ten months of training in the DC area sped by in a blur. The first half was spent in attaché training, my husband in one kind of school and me in another. I was learning diplomatic hostess duties, table and flower arranging, food presentation, and all the other little duties that would be a part of the attaché experience. There were quite a few of us wives—everyone whose husband was going to be an attaché in various countries all over the globe from every branch of the armed forces. We all got various tips on local customs and behaviors according to where we were being sent. We were also told stories of the "what not to do" variety. This would include not serving hamburger to people from India (the cow is sacred), not discussing Hitler's evil regime in the presence of the German attaché's wife (and don't seat her next to the Israeli wife at your luncheon), and not taking for granted that the domestics you hire really understand what you mean when you say, "Add a little garnish to the salad." One attaché wife averted a potential disaster when she realized that her maid had actually taken a packet of suppositories stored in the refrigerator because of the heat and cut them up into attractive little slices, which she had then added to the salad. Another wife had instructed her maid to "wash the outside of the refrigerator," only to come home later to find that the young girl, who couldn't have weighed more than 110 pounds, had actually pushed the appliance *outside* and was hosing it off in the courtyard. (The language barrier... you gotta love it!)

My husband's training, of course, was a little more detailed, and whenever I asked him what he learned in school that day, he would just smile and say, "If I tell you that, I'll have to kill you!" By the end of the training, we were calling each other Boris and Natasha, and I kept asking him when he was going to receive his "secret squirrel ring."

The second half of the training, the language school portion, wasn't quite as fun. From the minute we walked in the door, I felt out of my element. I am a visual learner, and everything in class was auditory. They never spoke English. The only language we ever heard was whatever we were supposed to be learning. For me, it was agony. The closest I had ever come to speaking Spanish was ordering at Taco Bell and repeating Arnold Schwarzenegger's "hasta la vista, baby," which, since he spoke with an Austrian accent, didn't get me any closer to my objective. I kept plugging away at it, though, but by the end, I realized that I just didn't have a natural affinity for languages. Zack did a lot better than I did, which was a good thing since his life and success as an attaché would depend on being able to speak and understand the language. By the time we were done, I was confident that I could say, "My name is..." "Where's the bathroom?" (imperative with two kids) and "I'll have fries with that please!" I was ready to go, or so I thought. What I wasn't ready for were the circumstances that would drive me to make one of the hardest decisions in my life.

For some reason that escapes me at the moment, we decided to drive to Mexico instead of fly. The minute we crossed over the border into Mexico—one heck of a drive from Washington DC I might add—I knew I was in trouble. The boys were getting car happy after such a long drive and weren't amused by my "let's count the burrows on the side of the road" game any longer. They had been begging for the bathroom. When we crossed over in Nuevo Laredo, Zack went to handle the necessary paperwork, and I said that I thought I could at least handle taking the boys to the bathroom. Wrong! I knew I was correct when I said, "Donde esta el bano?" but the rapid fire Spanish that came out of this man's mouth was *nothing* like I had heard in class. It was so fast I expected to see sparks flying out of his mouth. I stood there with my mouth hanging open, unable to decipher a single syllable the man had said.

The boys were each pulling on one arm begging, "What did he say, Mom? What did he say?"

I said "gracias" to the kind Mexican in front of me and mumbled something to the boys like, "A bush behind that building over there sounds like a good idea!" Why hadn't it ever occurred to me that just because I knew what question to ask didn't mean I would understand the answer? And what good was that? I was in trouble. The bush worked this time, but what would I do the next time?

As I was soon to learn, the language barrier was only the beginning of the adventures that awaited us. After we had been driving for a day and a half through the barren stretches of Mexico, it was amazing to suddenly arrive in this huge city, one of the biggest in the world, smack dab in the middle of nowhere. As the boys and I sat there trying to take it in, Zack began to tell us a little bit of the history of Mexico City. Apparently it was built on what was once a giant lake bed, which was why, he explained, Mexico City was susceptible to earthquakes.

"Cool," the boys both said at once. Earthquakes … cool? Nope, not for me. An earthquake was definitely one of those experiences I could stand to live without.

One of the first things we saw, but never got used to, were all the poor people begging in the streets. It was especially painful when it was children. Although we had been advised not to encourage them, we did end up giving them a few pesos whenever it felt safe to lower the windows and hand it to them. Safety was going to be an issue there. Zack had already sat me down and explained that Mexico City was a beautiful city, rich in history, but it was also one of the worst in the world for crime and pollution. He had purchased a gun before we left, something we had previously both been against with two young boys in the house, but now it seemed like a necessary evil.

When we finally arrived at our temporary apartment, we were all exhausted, a little overwhelmed, and ready for a good night's sleep. And boy, would we need it. In the course of the next few weeks, as we all got used to living in a foreign country, there were constant surprises around every corner. We had told the boys not to use the tap water to brush their teeth, and so far they had remembered. But keeping your mouth shut while you are in the shower is another matter, and within a month of arriving, Seth had amoebas and Cody had giardia, two of the more annoying little bacteria that can invade your system if you're not careful with the water, both resulting in misery and mad dashes to the bathroom. Zack had the odious task of carrying our "samples" to be tested at the clinic at the embassy. I was grateful that we had the clinic to go to and that we could get quick answers and whatever medicine we needed, all in the same day. I had been sending the samples in little jars in a brown paper bag, but then someone asked Zack what was in his "sack lunch." As a result, he told me to come up with a better method of transport.

We had been told that the safest thing to do about the water was to get it from the embassy well, which was tested daily for any little creatures we knew weren't supposed to be there. Unfortunately, this required that we drag two huge water containers, similar to what you might take camping, up to the embassy every couple of days to re-supply our water. Then we would put them in our car and hope that we could negotiate the potholes back home without the water spilling.

One day as I was bringing a friend back after a water run, we hit a bump, and her upright ten-gallon Gatorade cooler fell over, the lid rolled off, and a huge wave of water came crashing through the length of the mini-van, soaking everything in its path, including our shoes, when it finally all came to rest in two big puddles at our feet. We just looked at each other and laughed … what can you do? Either laugh or cry, and we chose to laugh. Of course Zack wasn't laughing quite as hard the next day when he actually had to remove the carpet from the van to get it to fully dry. To make matters worse, a volcano not too far from Mexico City decided to belch out some ash that day. We woke up in the morning to what looked like snow gently drifting down all over the yard. Ash and wet carpet make a muddy carpet, so we made a mad dash to try to drag the carpet under the carport.

Besides a belching volcano, Mother Nature had a few other tricks up her sleeve. We always knew that earthquakes were a possibility, but when we lay down to go to sleep at night, it was the last thing on our mind. Well, it quickly became the first thing when we were suddenly awakened in the middle of the night with our bed shaking back and forth and a low rumble of the earth filling our ears. I was terrified, never having been in one before, and the shaking seemed to be getting worse by the second. Next, our power went out (which was always iffy, even on the best of days), and Seth started yelling "Dad, Dad!" Zack jumped out of bed, negotiating a moving floor the best he could, and ran into the boys' room to comfort Seth. Cody, however, slept through the whole thing and was mad in the morning that he had missed all the excitement.

I curled up into a ball, pulled the covers over my head, and kept repeating to myself, "It will be over soon... it will be over soon." As I lay there with my eyes squeezed tightly shut, I could hear things rattling around on my dresser and the crystal down in my china cabinet clinking together. After what seemed like five minutes, but was really less than one, the shaking stopped. Seth calmed down once he realized it was over and nothing bad had happened. He fell back asleep pretty quickly, and Zack came back to bed. "Welcome to Mexico," he said as he crawled in beside me. He was asleep and snoring softly after less than three minutes, whereas I was lying there with my eyes wide open wondering how I had ever let him talk me into coming to this God-forsaken place with earthquakes, volcanoes, and amoebas in the water. (Everything seems worse at night.)

After we had been there for six months and we'd had several more small quakes, I can't say I was getting used to it, but it definitely wasn't as terrifying as the first time. We did have reason to be worried. On September 19, 1985, Mexico City suffered an 8.1 earthquake with devastating results. Over 9000 people were killed, over 30,000 were injured, 100,000 were left homeless, and scores of buildings were destroyed. I tried not to worry about another "big one" every time the earth started moving, but it was really never far from my mind.

Before we even arrived in Mexico, I had purchased a

lot of small American flags and also a flag for each country that had attaché representatives in Mexico with the idea that it would be neat to display them when we had guests over. There were over twenty-two countries that sent attachés to Mexico, with the US sending the highest number as each branch of the service was represented. For me it was a sign of respect and a small touch that I found people really appreciated when they came to our home.

I was a bit nervous before our first dinner party. I had a hard time deciding what to serve, then an even harder time finding some of the ingredients in the Mexican "tiendas" or "super mercados" for all my American dishes. It was also fun to try to describe in my broken Spanish to our maids how I wanted my recipes followed and served. At times it was easier just to do it myself, but then they became defensive, like I didn't trust them to do it right. I was also on the lookout to make sure that they washed their hands. They were not as cautious about the amoeba problem and drank the water freely. They were almost always taking medicine to get rid of them, but I couldn't watch them all the time.

Luckily, the invitations were printed out at the embassy, and we choose six couples that we thought would all be compatible (their countries weren't at war or didn't have any long-standing feuds going on). We set the date and everyone accepted, so we were ready, or at least as ready as we could be.

I soon learned that people from different countries had different ideas about what to wear for dinner, and we had people arrive in everything from casual pants and a golf shirt to a business suit and cocktail dress. I dressed somewhere in the middle hoping to make everyone feel comfortable. I realized that I had made a mistake of serving salad because too many people were wary of germs found in the lettuce over in Mexico. I had soaked everything in disinfectant specifically for fruit and vegetables, but still only about half of the guests ate their salad. The rest of the meal was a hit though, and we also learned that everyone else but us, it seemed, were big drinkers. We barely had enough wine to keep everyone happy. Luckily, several people had brought a bottle as a hostess gift. We went through far more than I thought we would, so another lesson learned.

Our first party was a success, and soon after we started to receive invitations to other people's homes. Normally this was not a problem, but we did have some things we had to adjust to. For one thing, many times the dinner hour was very late, preceded by a lengthy cocktail hour. I rarely, if ever, drink, and I was told that no matter how polite I was, declining might be considered an insult, especially if it was their native drink, like vodka at the Russian's house and tequila at the Mexican's house.

I remember one evening in particular. We had been invited to a Mexican's home in Cuernavaca, and they were very kind and gracious. The food was wonderful, they had a great mariachi band, and everyone was drinking, singing, and dancing, having a great time. After I had been handed my third tequila of the night with a wedge of lime by a very happy Mexican and told to drink up, I was looking for a plant that I could quietly pour the tequila into. For me, drinking tequila is akin to drinking kerosene. The minute I tried it, my throat was burning, my eyes were watering, and I couldn't speak for fifteen minutes. So I was not anxious to have another go; on the other hand, I didn't want to kill one of their plants either. I ended up dumping it in the grass. Zack, on the other hand, who was sacrificing himself for the spirit of good relations, had availed himself of quite a few shots of tequila and was feeling no pain.

The food was copious and good, and I tasted a bit of everything, even if I didn't know what it was. I was doing fine until they brought out the sautéed crickets. Zack motioned me over and said, "Here, honey, try the crickets.

They're sautéed in garlic, and they're great!" I gave him a look that said, "If you weren't out of your mind because of the tequila, you never would have offered me crickets, sautéed or otherwise!"

Right about then, somebody danced by me with a sombrero on, shaking a pair of maracas, and said, "Hey, be a good sport; eat the crickets!" (Obviously another tequila fan.) I turned around to find Zack scooping up a spoonful of crickets, dropping them in a tortilla, rolling it up, and popping it into his mouth. My stomach still turns when I remember the disgusting crunching sound it made while he chewed. But he had a big grin on his face, and all I could say was, "Maybe next time. But for now, maybe you should remove the cricket leg that is sticking out of your teeth and call that your last tequila!" Before he could respond, another happy reveler grabbed me from behind, and the next thing I knew, I was doing the Macarena with a Mexican admiral. At least it was better than eating crickets.

The longer we stayed, of course, the better my Spanish became, but I was still making very simple errors. One that we laugh about now but was mortifying for me at the time occurred when my parents flew down to visit us. We were invited to a lively cocktail party given by the Cubans, and we decided to take my parents along. As we entered the room and were greeted by a large crowd of attachés, I proudly announced in my best Spanish, "I would like you to meet my mother and my father." That's what I *thought* I said. In reality, what I said was, "I would like you to meet my mother and my potato." Everyone started to laugh, and I very quickly realized that I had just introduced my father as a vegetable. I was very red faced, but everyone was gracious. We had a great evening. People from many different countries came over to speak to and welcome my parents. They even ended up dancing with our attaché friends from Venezuela, and I never even knew that my dad could dance!

We enjoyed showing my parents around Mexico. We took them to the Pyramids of the Sun and the Moon at Teotihuacan, just outside Mexico City, where Zack, my dad, and the boys all climbed to the top while Mom and I waited at the bottom. We drove to Acapulco to do the tourist thing, and my parents were amazed at the glaring difference between the poor living in cardboard houses just blocks from high-rise resorts and luxury yachts. It was part of the fabric that makes up Mexico, but it was sad to see the children, especially, begging on the streets and dressed in ill-fitting clothes, dirty matted hair, and no shoes. I just wanted to scoop them up, take them back to the hotel, give them a warm bath and a good meal, and put them to sleep in a clean bed. But of course that wasn't possible, and much to our disappointment in ourselves, we actually began to get used to seeing and eventually ignoring the poverty all around us. I think it made an impression on Seth and Cody though, and I hope maybe it's an image that will stay with them for the rest of their lives.

Our time in Mexico was a mixture of fun, excitement, fear, and homesickness. I felt proud to be an American representing our country, but the hardships at times seemed overwhelming. There was the constant threat of assault and kidnapping, and I never got much sleep when Zack was traveling around Mexico on business. Two of the American attaché wives were held up at gun point at an ATM, one family had their car stolen—car seats and everything, and probably most traumatic of all, one of Zack's friends who worked at the American embassy and whom he saw every day was gunned down as he got out of a taxi in front of his home. All the thief got was his watch and $50 in Mexican currency, and for this an innocent American lost his life and left behind a wife and three young children. The man was never caught, and the incident barely made the Mexican newspapers. But for us it was a haunting reminder that

Mexico City is one of the most dangerous cities in the world and that we were Americans living in a foreign country.

Somewhere around the eighteen-month mark, I had a day that forced me to make one of the hardest decisions of my life. I had been fighting off a three-day nonstop headache because of the pollution, both boys were home sick (again), and we had just finished one of our busiest months ever, filled with a social engagement almost every night. Even though I knew this was part of the job when Zack agreed to become an attaché, I was weary of the whole thing. I hated leaving my children in the care of a nanny when they were sick, I hated that feeling of helplessness when the power went out and I couldn't reach my husband, and most of all I couldn't take the constant worry about our safety.

On this particular morning, we had just received word that there had been an attempted kidnapping of an American child off his school bus. Luckily this incident had occurred near the entrance to another embassy, and the armed guards had been able to stop the kidnappers and retrieve the child without injury to him or any of the other horrified students on the bus. But I had had enough. Zack tried to downplay it for my sake, but I could tell it bothered him too. Later that afternoon, as I stood with a cold rag on Cody's forehead while he vomited for the third time in as many hours, I realized that I just couldn't take it anymore.

I was tired of the constant worry about the kids since they seemed to be sick with one thing or another most of the time. I found myself missing reliable electricity, clean air, family, friends, and the familiarity of the United States. For the first time in our married life, I considered going home early without my husband. I knew that I had a duty to fulfill as an attaché wife representing our country, and in all the years we had been married and places we had moved, Zack and I had never lived apart. It was a hard decision, but I told my husband that I wanted to return home with the boys to the United States, even if it meant we would be apart for the last six months of his tour in Mexico. It killed me to do it, and in my weaker moments, I had to remind myself that I wasn't "leaving" my husband; I was leaving Mexico for the sake of our children.

We enjoyed our time in Mexico and made some wonderful friends. We traveled to places we never would have seen otherwise, but I was through; it was time to go home. It was a difficult decision for him too, but in the end, Zack agreed. The boys and I made plans to return home to the States and wait until this tour of duty was over. When our plane landed back in the United States and I could see our flag waving in the breeze, I was at peace again. The boys and I missed Zack terribly during those last six months, and of course I worried about his safety. But he had a job to do, and I understood that. I chalked up our time apart as just another one of the sacrifices that are required by military wives, every day, all over the world.

Whenever people ask me about our tour in Mexico, I always speak fondly of our time there because we did have some extraordinary experiences and Mexico is a beautiful country with warm and welcoming people. But in my heart, I will always look upon that as a time when I really learned to appreciate what it means to be an American and all the simple joys of daily life that we take for granted, like clean air and water, good schools, safe parks where our children can play, apple pie, and baseball. For all the travels this military life has brought us, it's helped to remind us how proud we are to be Americans, and like Dorothy said, "There's no place like home."

Audra
In Sickness and In Health

My husband is a hunk of a man. He stands 6'3" and has big broad shoulders, a narrow waist, and long muscular legs. He is a man's man. He likes football, working on his car, and doing projects around the house, as well as being the undisputed king of his domain—our home. Our family consists of two sons and their little miracle of a sister who came along many years after we were told our family would never get any bigger. From day one, she has been the apple of her father's eye. That's not to say that he isn't close to his sons; he is. But there is always this certain kind of gentleness that comes over him whenever he is around our daughter. He is so big, and she is so small. To see them together reminds me of all the different kinds of love that can exist between two people no matter how different they are.

The relationship that my husband has with our sons is different. It is relaxed, rough and tumble, and full of sports games of one kind or another. If my husband isn't coaching their teams, whenever possible he is there on the sidelines, encouraging them and giving advice and praise. He stands head and shoulders above most of the other fathers, and the boys are always proud to say, "That's my dad!"

My name is Audra, and my husband's name is Spence. He is a Green Beret, a division of the army that is thought by some to be a breed apart, which is one of the reasons they call them Special Forces. Their training is extreme, challenging every man to reach farther than he thinks he can possibly go. Many don't make it through the program, and those that do know that they will be given tough, dangerous missions to complete, anywhere at any time.

We accept that Spence goes away for weeks at a time and can never tell us where he is going. The old line "I can't tell you that or I will have to kill you" is used jokingly in our house all the time. Life for Spence has been golden. He graduated top of his class at West Point, did his Green Beret training, advanced in rank, got challenging, high-profile jobs, and felt like a success in every aspect of his life. But sometimes, I think God looks down and says, "Our good and faithful servant has walked the path of righteousness, but his path has been without obstacles. Let us test the faith of this man, this family, to see if he remains strong in darkness as well as in light." So God decided to test us, and that's where this story begins.

Spence was going to Afghanistan. Our sons, Riley and Rance, were fourteen and sixteen respectively, and our little Renata was four. He had about a two-week warning where we crammed as much fun into our lives as we could. My parents came to stay with the kids, and Spence and I took a quick trip alone together and walked on the beach in the moonlight, picking up shells, tossing them into the ocean, and chasing each other in circles. When we got back to the cottage we had rented, Spence picked me up in his arms and carried me over the threshold, just like it was our honeymoon. We awoke early to watch the sunrise, and it was so beautiful, we were speechless. After a few moments, Spence looked down into my eyes and told me that this memory would be burned into his brain forever. We never spoke of the idea that Spence might not come back, but it was always there, just under the surface. For this precious weekend, we had each other and life was perfect.

The next weekend, Spence and I took the boys and Renata camping. It was one of our favorite family activities. We went to our favorite spot near a large lake and went fishing, hiked on the Appalachian Trail, and sang songs around the fire. We roasted marshmallows, made s'mores, and had a great time. We let the boys stay out of school for an extra day, and come Monday afternoon, nobody wanted to leave our quiet little piece of heaven. But we did, and Tuesday morning, Spence left.   Things got back to a normal routine around our house. The boys were busy at school and with their various activities. Renata and I enjoyed our time together at home. She would be turning five in the summer and would be starting kindergarten in the fall, and I wanted as much time with her as I could get. She missed her daddy though, and we spent a fair amount of time drawing pictures for him. I would always try to enclose a photo or two in each letter that we sent since I felt like Renata and the boys were growing and changing so quickly and I didn't want Spence to miss out on it. I didn't know exactly where he was or how often he would get his mail, but we sent it on knowing (hoping) that he would get it eventually.

Spence was due to be gone for roughly six months. He had already been gone for six weeks when I received a call. I remember that once I realized it was a military person calling to tell me something about Spence, my heart jumped to my throat, but I was sure that if he was dead, they would not deliver that kind of news over the phone. And I was right. He was not dead, but he was gravely injured. They could not tell me the details of his injury or how it was sustained, but they did say he was stable and would be transferred home as soon as it was medically feasible. I was given a POC, or point of contact, and told that I would be given an update as soon as it was available. I asked if there was any way that I could speak to Spence, and they told me, "Not now. He is heavily sedated, awaiting transfer to a larger hospital."

I thanked the man and slowly hung up the phone. I could hear Renata upstairs playing house with her baby dolls, chattering away. The boys were due home from school in a little over an hour. Rance had wrestling practice after school that day, and I wanted the boys to be together when I broke the news about their dad. I sat there feeling numb for a few minutes and didn't even realize that my hands were clasped, very tightly, in my lap. After a few minutes of staring into space, I called and sent a message for both boys to come home right away after school. I can't remember what I did in those minutes in between learning about Spence and calling the school, but before I knew it, the boys were home. Rance was furious with me for making him miss his wrestling practice so close to a match.

"Mom, you can't do this to me!" Rance yelled as he slammed the front door. "What the hell is so important that we needed to come home right after school? I have a match this weekend!"

Rance's tirade shocked me back to reality, and I immediately told him to watch his language and his tone of voice. I told the boys to go into the kitchen and that I would be right there to talk to them. I wanted to make sure that Renata was distracted while I spoke with the boys. When I came into the kitchen, both boys had grabbed a Coke and a bag of Cheetos and were waiting at the table. Riley looked curious and slightly concerned; Rance just looked mad. All he could think about was missing his practice. I guess the thought hadn't even occurred to him that there might be something wrong.

As I sat down, Riley said, "What's up, Mom?"

I took a deep breath, glanced out the window, and told the boys that I had received a call about their dad.

I saw a flicker of fear pass over their faces, and Rance said right away, "He's not dead, is he?"

Riley looked from his brother to me, and I was quick to assure them that he was alive but had been badly injured. They were silent for a moment, and then they both began firing off questions, none of which I had the answers to. I didn't know exactly what was wrong, if his injuries were life threatening, how he sustained them, or what it all meant. Riley said that maybe it wasn't so bad … maybe just a broken leg or something. But I had a feeling it was much more than that. I told the boys that we would just have to wait until someone called us again to give us more information.

The wait, it turned out, was an excruciating twenty-four hours. The boys asked to stay home from school the next day, and I let them. We had finally received a call from a corpsman who said that the doctor who had been attending to Spence would be calling us around 1:00 in the afternoon.

I spent the day trying to do normal things around the house. I suddenly felt the need to get everything clean and in order. The boys were quiet; they lay on their beds for a while, played with Renata a little, and went outside to shoot hoops but found that their hearts weren't in it and came back inside. Around noon, I sat down with the boys to have lunch; Renata was taking a nap. I tried to reassure them that whatever had happened to Dad, we would handle it the best we could as a family. We said a quick prayer for strength and then began the minute-by-minute wait for the phone to ring.

One o'clock came and went, and my nerves were on edge when the phone finally rang. There was a delay in the connection, but the voice was clear. A man introduced himself as the physician who had examined Spence. He began by saying that he felt that Spence was no longer in immediate danger of dying from the wounds he had received. I was relieved and tears came to my eyes. Both boys were standing nearby, so I shook my head to let them know that I wasn't crying because of some terrible news. They stood by anxiously as the doctor proceeded to explain my husband's situation.

He began by saying that Spence's legs had been badly damaged to the point that neither one could be saved. One was amputated just above the knee and the other just below the knee. After hearing this, I must have become quite pale, because Rance pulled out a chair for me, and I sat down just as my legs started to feel wobbly. I listened to the doctor as he described some of the things that were done to try and save his legs, but in the end, they were too badly damaged. I asked if Spence knew about his condition, and the doctor replied that he had not been told yet because he was still heavily sedated after the surgery.

The doctor had said that Spence had suffered two major injuries, and as of yet he had not been specific about the second. I couldn't imagine that anything could be worse than the loss of his legs, but I felt compelled to ask him to tell me what other injuries he had. For the first time, the doctor sounded hesitant, as if he was trying to figure out the best way to tell me what was next. He said that he realized that all of this was a shock and that it would take time, but that Spence could still lead a happy, fulfilling life. I began to feel a sense of panic … why did he feel the need to reassure me before he told me what else was wrong with Spence? If he was trying to soften the blow, forget it; I just wanted to know what we were facing.

He was silent for a moment before he said, "Mrs. Ackerman, I'm afraid your husband has also lost the use of his eyes." His words hung in the air. With no thought of the boys standing right beside me, I blurted out, "You mean he's blind?" The shocked look on the boys' faces was immediate, and Riley's eyes filled with tears. This certainly wasn't the way I had wanted to break the news to the boys; in fact, I had been careful not to even repeat that his legs were gone, thinking that I could tell them gently after the call. But the minute I heard Spence was blind, I lost all sense of time and space and who was around me. All I could hear was the word "blind" ringing in my ears.

"Is this condition permanent? I mean is there any hope that he will ever see again?"

The doctor replied that no, there was no hope for any appreciable change in the future. I couldn't really tell you what the rest of the conversation was because my mind was stuck on that one word ... blind. Spence was blind. He would never be able to look at me or the children again. He would never know what Renata looks like as she grows, he'd never be able to watch the boys play sports again, drive a car, watch television, or ... the thoughts were coming at me faster than I could handle. I managed to get through the rest of the conversation somehow, and when I put the receiver down, I was vaguely aware that someone would be calling me to arrange transportation for me to fly to be with Spence. The doctor felt that someone should be with him when he received the news about his legs and his eyesight.

I was numb. I sat there staring straight ahead until I remembered the boys. I looked at their stricken faces as they took in the news that their dad was blind. I still had to tell them that he had also lost his legs. I felt this couldn't be happening. How could our lives have changed so drastically after one phone call? The boys were horrified when I told them the details, and all of us sat there, tears streaming down our faces, too shocked to even speak.

I waited a while to tell Renata and decided that a gentle version of the truth would be enough for her for the time being. I just told her that Daddy had hurt his legs and his eyes and that he would be coming home so we could take care of him. As my eyes welled with tears yet again, Renata softly patted my hand and said, "Don't worry, Mommy, I will help you take good care of Daddy."

The next few days were difficult. The boys were numb and quiet. I longed to be more of a comfort to them, but they didn't seem to want it and were both dealing with the news in their own way. There had been difficult phone calls to make to Spence's mom and my parents. I had arranged for Spence's sister to be with their mother when I made the call, and I was glad I did because Spence's mom, who could be difficult on the best of days, howled and wailed when I told her. I tried to comfort her the best I could but found I just didn't have the patience for her hysterics, not when I had my own children, my husband, and our future to worry about. When she wailed that he would be better off dead than a blind cripple, I knew I had to get off the phone. His sister quickly got on and said she was sorry about her mother and that she would handle her. I thanked her and hung up, furious at what his mother had said. Even in her old age and grief, how could she say something like that? So you can imagine my shock when later that night, our oldest son, Rance, expressed the same sentiment.

"Dad wouldn't want to live like that, Mom. He won't be able to do anything. Maybe it would have been better if he had just died."

I couldn't believe what I was hearing.

"Rance, you can't mean that. Dad is still Dad. He hasn't lost his mind, his personality, or his love for us. Having him here with us, no matter what his condition, is better than not having him at all. And when he comes home, he is going to need all the support we can give him. I'm not saying it won't be hard; it will be. But we can never think he would be better off dead."

I could tell he had been doing a lot of thinking about all of this when he looked me right in the eye and said,

"Have you really considered what it's going to be like for you, Mom? You will have to take complete care of him for the rest of your lives! He is supposed to be the one taking care of you!"

I appreciated his concern but was surprised that he felt this way. I went on to assure him that being married to someone you love doesn't give you any guarantees that life will always be everything you want it to be.

"If something happened to me, don't you think Daddy would take care of me?"

"Yes, but it's not the same."

I leaned in and took his hand, something that at the age of sixteen I hadn't done in a while.

"Rance, listen to me. We love Dad and that hasn't changed. We will cope, Dad will adjust to these changes, and life will go on. Will it be the same? No, it won't. I'm not saying it will be easy; it will be the hardest thing that any of us has ever faced. But we can do it, okay?"

Rance looked into my face to see if I really believed what I was saying, and he seemed satisfied with what he saw there. I knew that I was trying to convince myself as much as I was my son. I had no idea what we would be facing. I knew that great strides had been made with the use of artificial limbs, but I had no idea how we would learn to cope with his blindness. I had never even met or known anyone who was blind, and that was what scared me the most.

Little Renata had gotten lost in the shuffle of the next few days. People were coming and going from the house, some bringing meals or stopping by to offer their support. Riley had taken it upon himself to look after his little sister. It gave him something to do and was a huge help to me as I prepared to fly to see Spence. Renata was blissfully unaware of the harsh reality of the situation; she knew only what I had explained to her earlier, that Daddy was hurt at his work and was coming home. There would be time to fill in the details later as she was face to face with them. But for now, she knew all she needed to know.

My parents arrived to stay with the kids, and I finally found myself on the long flight to Washington DC, alone for the first time in days. All I wanted to do was get to Spence, touch him, kiss him, and tell him that everything would be all right. He had been in and out of sedation but never awake enough to ask any questions. I tried to imagine how he was going to respond, but I couldn't bear to think of his finding out exactly what he had lost. I just closed my eyes and prayed that God would help me to be all that I needed to be for my husband and my children, and before I knew it, out of sheer exhaustion, I fell into a deep and soundless sleep.

In what seemed like just a few moments later, someone was tapping me on the shoulder asking me if I wanted anything to drink before we began our descent into Reagan National Airport in Washington DC. I asked for a glass of water since I was feeling a little dry and made a quick stop at the restroom. When I got off the plane, I felt somewhat refreshed but had a growing sense of fear in the pit of my stomach. How would I handle it when I saw my husband? It had been almost two months since I last saw him, tall, strong, and whole. I pushed the frightening scenario from my mind and made my way into the terminal.

My plane came into terminal C, which was fairly new and still looked good. The smell from the various restaurants made me realize that I was getting hungry. I had slept most of the way, even though now the most you can expect refreshment-wise on a flight is a little bag of peanuts and a soft drink. A glass of wine had been tempting, but I needed to be clear headed and totally in control.

After I retrieved my bag, I headed outside to catch a cab to the Walter Reed Army Hospital. I was surprised to see a nicely dressed woman, roughly my age, holding a sign with my name on it: A. Ackerman. I approached her and asked if she was waiting for me, Audra Ackerman, and she said yes. I hadn't realized that there would be anyone waiting for me. She quickly explained that she was a volunteer who often times met family members when they were coming to DC to first see their loved ones who had been injured overseas.

"Washington is a beautiful city, but it can be a little hectic and confusing. We like to be there for the family members when they are making such a difficult trip, especially if they are alone, like you are," she said. She introduced herself as Carol, showed me her military dependent ID card, which was just like mine, and said she would be taking me to the hospital if that was all right with me. I readily agreed and was grateful to have someone else do the thinking for me for a little while longer before I saw Spence.

Carol dropped me off at the main entrance of a very large and imposing hospital. She told me to go on into the visitor's desk and that she would join me as soon as she parked the car. I signed in and realized that my hands were shaking, and I was glad to see Carol's new yet familiar face coming around the corner. I felt so afraid and was grateful for the service that the members of her group, both officer and enlisted wives, provided. She said that she was available to stay with me for a little longer, or if I felt more comfortable going on alone, she would direct me to the correct floor and leave me. I hesitated, not sure exactly what I wanted, when she smiled and said, "I don't mind staying with you a little longer, if I could be of any help to you."

I nodded and said that I would appreciate it. Her conversation was light; she didn't press me for details about my husband's situation but did tell me to ask any questions that I might have. She would try and help me find the answers. The only thing I could think to say was that I would need to be made aware of what type of help was available to military personnel who were gravely injured like my husband.

She said that a counselor and a chaplain would be available to speak with us about our options for rehabilitation and long-term care, both of which sounded scary and depressing to me.

As I walked down the hall to Spence's room, I saw several men in the halls, displaying various types of injuries. One was so young that he looked barely older than Rance. He was quick to smile and tip his head to me when I smiled at him, and suddenly, all I wanted to do was to see Spence.

It's hard to say exactly how I felt the first moment I saw my husband. He was lying flat on his back in a neatly made bed, and I immediately took comfort in the familiarity of his face, his big, broad chest, and those beautiful arms that just two months ago had carried me across the threshold of that beach house and were now lying straight down at his side. I paused for a moment to take in the sight of him, allowing my eyes to rest on his legs. They had placed a kind of small tent apparatus over the lower half of his legs, so I couldn't really see them. I learned later that this was to help keep the pressure of the sheets off his freshly bandaged legs. There was a band of gauze across both eyes that stretched around the back of his head. It was much smaller than I thought it would be, and it looked like he had just been shaved and had his hair washed.

I was touched for a moment, thinking that someone had taken the time to make him look his best before I arrived. I wondered if Spence knew someone had walked into the room. (Carol had stayed behind at the nurses' station, and a nurse was waiting outside his door while I tiptoed in.)

Just then Spence turned his head slightly to his left as if he'd heard me and said in a familiar voice, "Audra, is that you?" My eyes welled with tears at the sound of his voice, and I dropped my purse and rushed to his side.

"Yes, it's me," I said in a voice shaky with relief. "I'm here, Spence, I'm here." He reached his left arm out to me and pulled me close to his chest, and I leaned in and kissed him gently on the lips. "I don't want to hurt you," I said as the tears continued to roll down my cheeks. His response broke my heart.

"The only thing you could ever do to hurt me is to leave me, and I understand if you do. There isn't much left to stay for."

His words were more of a shock to me than the sight of him lying in his hospital bed. We had always been so close and so happy, and it was inconceivable that either of us would ever even think something like that, no matter what the circumstances. I told him that I never wanted to hear him say anything like that ever again.

"You're still you and I'm still me. This doesn't change anything."

He was silent for several minutes. I wondered if he had fallen asleep when I noticed that the bandages over his eyes had become wet, and I realized he was crying. Even though he hadn't made a sound, I suddenly realized what a relief it must have been for him to hear me say that I would never leave him and that his injuries would never change the way I felt about him. How awful it must have been for him, laying there waiting, wondering, not knowing how I would react, fearing he might spend the rest of his life broken and alone. It was more than I could bear to think about.

I laid my head gently down, and after a few minutes I realized with the steady rise and fall of his chest that he had fallen asleep. I knew that no matter what Spence and I would face in our future, nothing could ever make me love him less than I did in that moment. I thanked God, not for the first time or the last, for bringing him into my life.

I wouldn't be telling the truth if I said that things from that day forward were easy; they weren't, and in ways I never could have imagined. I was disappointed that I had not been there with Spence when they told him the extent of his injuries. But he had awoken and demanded to know his situation, so they told him. I knew it would take him a while (although exactly how long I wasn't certain) to adjust to all that had happened to him and all the ways it would change his life. I knew that there would be a lengthy period of healing and rehabilitation. He would probably need to learn Braille and to use a cane, if he could even walk. And then there were the more practical aspects, like what we would need to do to our home to make accommodations for a wheelchair. Thankfully, our master bedroom was on the main level, but the door to our bathroom was too small for a wheelchair to pass through. What would we do?

As time wore on and Spence slowly began to heal in the hospital, I became aware of all the ways this would affect our lives, and the questions were endless. Would Spence ever be able to work again? How would we get by? How would the children, especially the boys who were used to their father being so involved in their sports activities, adjust to the changes in their father's physical limitations? How would I react when Spence was finally able to come home and I needed to help him change the bandages on his stumps? Could I do it? How would I take over doing all the things that he now wasn't able to do and still make him feel like the head of our family?

Every day these questions and a hundred more swam through my head. I couldn't really talk to Spence about my fears; it was all he could do to cope with the almost constant pain he was in. He suffered two or three excruciating migraines a week, and although the ophthalmologist assured us that these should eventually ease off, it didn't make them any easier to bear until then. But by far the hardest thing for Spence to deal with was the almost constant "phantom" pain he experienced. He understood that his legs were gone, but apparently his nerve endings didn't. It was maddening to him to experience the feeling of pain in legs that weren't even there. It wasn't logical and he couldn't control it, so he fought against it.

All of this was compounded by the fact that his world was dark. He couldn't see me, himself, or what was left of his legs, and many days during my visits, I would find him angry and despondent. Even the simple task of getting the food from his plate to his mouth without spilling it down his front was a challenge.

He missed the kids, wanted to come home, and was frustrated with his body's inability to do what needed to be done before they would release him. He needed to be able to take care of his stumps until they were healed enough for him to be fitted with prosthetic legs. He would have to be content with learning to get around in a wheelchair until then. Since he couldn't see where he was going, this would require some assistance. The bandages around his eyes had long since been removed, but because of the burst blood vessels that made the whites of his eyes blood red, he chose to wear sunglasses, sensitive to how his appearance might frighten or repel people, especially our children.

Rance and Riley had both wanted to come and see their dad in the hospital, but Spence didn't want the kids to see him there. He felt that all the changes in him would be shocking enough, and they were better off coming to terms with it at home.

Finally at long last I was able to take him home. He had made some friends there in the hospital, and he promised to stay in touch with several of them. We were both grateful to the nursing staff that had been so kind and attentive during the many weeks of his recovery. Now it was time to leave the security of the hospital and make it on our own.

As the orderly wheeled Spence out into the sunshine, I couldn't help but notice how handsome my husband still was. He was a little thinner, and his hair was longer than he normally kept it. But he was still a striking figure, even in a wheelchair, and suddenly, my spirits soared. We were finally going home, and whatever happened beyond that, I was sure I could handle.

The orderly showed him the easiest way to slide from the wheelchair into the back seat of the cab. Spence had developed quite a bit of strength in his upper arms just from hoisting himself in and out of bed and into the wheelchair. Although quite a bit of Spence's 6'3" frame had come from his legs, he was still tall in a sitting position, and his head was only an inch from the roof of the taxi.

When I commented to him what a beautiful day it was, he smiled only slightly and said, "Is it? I guess I'll just have to take your word for it." I bit my tongue for having said something that might have been insensitive, but I realized that we couldn't change the normal expressions we used every day and that Spence would just have to get past the small stuff. When I slipped my hand into his, he squeezed it and smiled, maybe realizing that he had been a little snippy with his response. We were both in unfamiliar territory, but we had time and each other. For now, that would have to see us through.

By the time we arrived at the airport, got a wheelchair, and navigated our way through security and to our gate, we were both exhausted. Spence commented that he had never realized all the sounds around him that he took for granted when he had sight. Now everything he heard was his primary source of defining what was all around him, and I think after a while the noise of the airport became a little overwhelming for him.

Before long, we were safely seated in first class (Luckily we were able to upgrade so Spence had more room.). Spence had his sunglasses on and a blanket across his lap, so his injuries weren't obvious to the casual observer. We were lucky in that this particular airline had a small, square stool on wheels that fit easily down the aisle so Spence was able to lift himself from his wheelchair on to the stool and then from the stool into his seat. I don't know how we would have gotten him to his seat with such a narrow aisle without it. I made a mental note to make sure this accommodation was available whenever we flew.

We settled in for the flight, me at the window and Spence in the aisle seat, and we both dozed off. Unfortunately, it didn't last for long. Apparently we weren't the only ones who got upgrades. A young sergeant was seated directly across from Spence and while waiting for the flight had been hanging out at the airport bar. He was speaking in a loud and obnoxious voice, demanding to be served another cocktail. The flight attendant knew that he had already had too much and was politely declining his request, but he was becoming belligerent. I could see that Spence was wide awake and listening closely to the scene.

"I just got back from Afghanistan, and I deserve another drink. And I want it *now!*"

I could tell that the flight attendant was getting nervous, but she was holding her ground.

"I'm sorry, sir, but I'm not going to serve you any alcohol. However, I would be happy to get you a can of juice or a soft drink."

Suddenly the sergeant undid his seat buckle and jumped up into the aisle. Spence's head moved right with him, and you wouldn't have had any idea he couldn't see what was happening. With his head looking up directly where the man was standing, Spence said in a firm and quiet voice, "Sergeant, I suggest you take her offer of a non-alcoholic drink and sit down."

I had no idea how Spence knew he was a sergeant. I knew he couldn't see him, but for all the world, you never would have known at that moment that Spence was blind.

"Who are you to tell me to sit down?" the man yelled at Spence.

Before I or the sergeant knew what was happening, Spence's right arm shot out and grabbed the front of the man's uniform, and Spence said in a stronger, louder voice, "I'm Lieutenant Colonel Spence Ackerman, and *I* just got back from Afghanistan too. I'm telling you to sit down and shut up, or your commanding officer will be the first call I make when I get off this plane. You got it, Sergeant?"

Spence was in civilian clothes and his hair was not cut in his normal, short military style, so I'm sure the man at first had no idea that Spence was an officer. The sergeant quickly looked Spence over (who still had a tight grip on his shirt) and decided wisely to back down. I wasn't sure if it was his rank or the fact that from the waist up Spence was solid muscle that made the sergeant apologize and sit down, but I was impressed and proud of my husband. The flight attendant was profoundly grateful.

The rest of the flight was quiet. It may have been my imagination, but it seemed like Spence was sitting a little taller in his seat. As I laid my head on his shoulder, I realized, *Sometimes a lion just has to make sure he can still roar.*

Arriving home was a different matter. Emotions ranged from weepy (me) to scared (Riley), mad (Rance), and curious (Renata). Of course Spence came into the house in a wheelchair, which was a bit of a shock for the kids. By then I was used to it, but for the kids it was a frightening idea that their dad had to be in that chair. I was momentarily glad that Spence couldn't see their faces since both boys were rooted to the spot as Spence was wheeled in, unsure what to say or do.

Sensing their initial awkwardness, I told the boys, "It's okay to come and hug Dad. You won't hurt him." Renata didn't need a second invitation because she took off across the kitchen at a run. Spence must have heard her little feet coming because he leaned forward, put his arms out, scooped her up and over his still sore legs (what was left of them), and hugged her close.

"Daddy!" she squealed. I closed my eyes for a moment and silently thanked God for her youth and her unabashed love for her daddy. It definitely helped to break the tension. After a minute or two, I lifted Renata off Spence's lap, and my father stepped forward and gave him a hearty pat on the back and a welcome home. My mother then stepped up, gave her son-in-law a kiss on the cheek, and said how good it was to have him back and that the children had been waiting anxiously. I saw my father gently push Riley, our younger son, forward, and he leaned down, gave Spence an awkward hug, and said, "Hi, Dad."

"Hi, son. How's it going?"

Riley hesitated for a moment, still staring down at the blanket where Spence's legs and feet should be. I gave him a look like, "Answer him!" Riley then stammered, "Uh…everything is good. School is good, you know…uh…everything is good."

Spence was looking directly where Riley was standing and said with a half smile, "Good, I'm glad to hear it."

At that point we all expected Rance to speak to his dad, but one look at him made me wonder if he could do it. He was white as a sheet and rooted to the spot. He hadn't moved since Spence and I had come into the kitchen.

"Rance…you here?" Spence asked. His head was cocked to one side, obviously listening for any sound of his oldest child. Spence was waiting for him to speak so he would know which direction to look.

Rance cleared his throat and said, "Yes, Dad, I'm here."

"Well, come here and shake my hand, son. I won't bite." He stuck out his hand, waiting for Rance to come and shake it, but Rance just couldn't do it. He was paralyzed. After a few seconds, Spence lowered his hand and realized that

Rance wasn't coming. All eyes were on our son, and I was mortified that he was doing this to his dad.

"Rance—" I started to say, when I was interrupted by Renata, who, with her hands on her little hips, marched over to Rance, pulled on his arm, and said, "Come on, Wance … you bein' a mean boy! Daddy's home!"

Apparently this was enough to shame Rance into stepping up and shaking his dad's hand. "Sorry, Dad, I am just getting over a cold, and I didn't want to make you sick."

It sounded lame even to me, but Spence shook his hand and said, "That's okay, son. I appreciate you thinking of me."

Spence's words were calm and understanding, but I could tell he was hurt. My mother asked Spence if he was hungry, and he replied that no, he was just tired and wanted to lie down before dinner. I offered to help get him settled, but he told me to go spend time with Renata since I had been gone for several weeks. Thankfully my dad had seen to it that doorways were enlarged, so when Spence got used to maneuvering around the house, he would be able to wheel right into our bedroom. I wheeled him in to our room then left him to go be with Renata. The door to our bathroom was not done, however, so Spence had no choice but to get down out of his wheelchair and scoot on his behind to the toilet. I know it was demeaning for him, and I thought more than once that first week that I would be glad for his sake when he got his artificial legs.

After about a half an hour, I went to check on him and found him sitting on the floor of our bathroom, tears streaming down his face. "I can't even reach the damn sink to wash my hands," he spat out. I tried to comfort him by reminding him that things might be a little difficult at first until we got everything sorted out, but we would manage. He was hurt and frustrated, and I could hardly blame him. It had been a grueling trip physically, then to come home and have his own son afraid to shake his hand, and being unable to even wash his hands at his own bathroom sink was too much. I knew it had been a bad day, and I wondered to myself how many more like this we had coming. What I should have also been worried about were the nights.

Almost nightly, Spence would thrash around in our bed, yelling things that were unintelligible and agonizing over the phantom pains in his legs. The doctors were trying to wean him off the many drugs he had used in the hospital, and the result was that his "night terrors" were getting worse instead of better. Every time it was the same—he would wake up drenched in sweat with his chest heaving and fists clenching the sheets. The first night at home was the worst. He woke the entire house. Renata was crying. My dad and Rance came running in our room after they heard Spence yelling, and it took me a good ten minutes to calm him down. Sitting up in bed with just his underwear on, Spence looked the same, well built and muscled. But because he was half delirious and didn't know Rance was in the room, he threw off the bed sheets, revealing his bandaged stumps.

Rance looked horrified. I yelled at him to get me some cold wet towels, and my dad moved to the door to head off Riley, who by that time was headed into the bedroom to see what was wrong. Thankfully my mother had gone into Renata's room, and she was back asleep in no time. But I wondered how in the world I would have handled the situation if I had been alone with just Spence and the kids. No sooner had the thought left my mind when Rance appeared with the cold towels, and as I was standing beside the bed ready to put the towel on his dad's forehead, Spence leaned over and threw up all over my nightgown. Actually, crazy as it might seem, I was just thankful that he hadn't hit our white carpet or my new comforter.

When I came back from changing, I found Rance wiping down his dad's neck and chest, saying calm, quieting words to him, and I knew we had passed a major hurdle. A moment of crisis had forced Rance to come to his dad's aid and put aside whatever fears he had about how his dad had changed. As I stood there watching my son care for his dad, I realized that we had forgotten Spence's 2:00 a.m. pain pill, which was probably the reason he became so ill. I brought Spence the pill and some lukewarm water to drink, and within twenty minutes, he was calm and asleep. Rance just stood there staring at him.

"Mom, I don't understand how Dad can feel pain in legs that aren't even there anymore."

I told him that I knew it seemed strange, but it was a fairly common phenomenon called phantom pain that hopefully with time would get better. I went on to explain, since Rance seemed receptive, that his dad would be fitted with artificial legs and would be walking again.

"I know, Mom. It's not his legs…it's his eyes. I can't bear the idea that he can't see."

"Well, if he can bear it, then we should be able to bear it," I said. "But I know it's all a shock, Rance. Everyone just needs time to adjust…you, me, Dad, the whole family. But he is going to need all of us, okay?"

Rance looked down at the sleeping form of his father, and tears came to his eyes.

"I'm sorry about earlier today, Mom…I just couldn't handle seeing him without his legs…with those sunglasses on and everything…I'm sorry."

I reassured my son that it was okay and thanked him for his help. Spence slept peacefully for the rest of the night, but that was to be the first of many tortured nights, which inevitably ended with me wondering if it was the psychological scars rather than the physical ones that were going to keep Spence from being whole again.

He never talked about the night he stepped on the land mine. I only know that he was attempting to retrieve two men from his platoon who had accidentally headed off into an area that they didn't know was heavily mined. One of the young men made it out, and the other, who raced to Spence's side after he was wounded, died beside him. The boy who died was only nineteen years old, just three years older than our own son. I know his name was Dane because every once in a while, I heard Spence trying to comfort the boy in his sleep, saying things like, "Hold on, Dane, help is coming … help is coming." Help did eventually come for Spence, but it was too late for Dane. I know it weighs heavily on my husband every day.

I wish I could say that life returned to normal for us, but it really never has. We had to create a new "normal." Spence went through countless doctors' appointments, rehab sessions, and fittings for his new legs. It was a wonderful sight when Spence first stood up to his full height again after receiving his artificial legs. It gave him the ability to walk, but he still couldn't see where he was going. So his next mountain to climb was to learn to walk with a cane and to read Braille. This was a bit harder, but Spence was determined. His hands were so large and the raised dots were so small, at first he feared he would never get the hang of it. The children were always willing to read to him, especially the boys, who had gotten into the habit of sitting down with their dad to read and discuss the sports page of the newspaper. But he stuck with it and eventually got the hang of it, and it gave him great joy to be able to sit down and read a story to Renata again.

Renata was a joy through the whole, long process. She liked to play nurse with her daddy, which could range anywhere from kissing his sightless eyelids to putting band-aids on his "hurt legs" to continually wanting to feed him chicken soup.

His greatest frustration was not being able to watch Rance and Riley play sports. After some trial and error, we realized that wrestling, Rance's favorite sport, was quite suitable for visually impaired people. So much of the skill in this sport is reading the other person's body language and movements through close body contact that being blind isn't really that much of a disadvantage. It wasn't long before Spence realized that if he took his artificial legs off and got down on the floor, he gave Rance a formidable opponent with whom to practice Sometimes Rance would even wear a blindfold just so they would be more evenly matched. Many a Saturday afternoon was spent with Spence and the boys trying out new moves and wrestling the day away.

Spence, determined to keep his "six pack" from turning into a "keg," had a portion of our basement turned into a weight room. And I have to say … he looked great! I began to worry a little bit about my own figure; he couldn't see it, but he could feel it. He was never anything other than complimentary and loving, but I still wanted to look my best for him, even if he couldn't see me.

A year or so after his injury, Spence was able to return to work part time for the Department of Defense in their National Security Agency. His job was to listen to and transcribe top-secret radio transmissions since he was fluent in Farsi, Urdu, and Arabic. It gave him a sense of purpose and allowed him to continue to earn a living for his family. Spence made full-bird colonel before he retired, and even though his career and his life took a path far different than he ever could have imagined, he made it work. We all did. Were there bad days, days when he wondered why this had happened to him or times when he cursed the darkness because he so much wanted to watch a sunrise or look into my face again? Yes, of course there were, and there continue to be to this day. But when Spence was asked to be a guest speaker for graduation at his alma mater, West Point, and the children and I sat in the audience as he began to speak, I saw a man standing proud, looking out on an audience that he could not see and delivering a speech that touched the hearts and minds of every young man at that ceremony. Every one of them was full of courage, pride, and hope for their future as they began the journey of serving their great country. As I thought back on the horrible words that Spence's mother had uttered that day that seemed so long ago, saying Spence would be better off dead than being blind and crippled, I looked around and realized that any one of these men would be blessed indeed to be called even half the man that was standing before them right now. Blessed, indeed.

Brook

WE'RE MOVING ... AGAIN

For the last twenty-three years, I have been married to the military.

Actually, I have been married to a wonderful man named Alex. Since he eats, sleeps, and breathes all things military, I have spent almost all of those twenty-three years feeling like I'm sharing my husband with a mistress that's even more demanding than I am, that mistress of course being the military. Alex comes from a long line of dedicated military men who have based their lives around service to their country. That also means that there was a long line of military wives that have been there with them, trying to hold it all together for the sake of honor, pride, patriotism, and of course love. There is no doubt that I love my country almost as much as I love my husband. Since I don't have the slightest desire to be an active part of the military myself (although many women do, and that's great), I decided that my best contribution to our country would be as a military wife and mother.

For all intents and purposes, I can honestly say that I have thrown myself into the job of being a military wife with as much energy and enthusiasm as I could muster on any given day. It hasn't always been easy. It's a difficult lifestyle, and not everybody can hack it. Sadly, the rate of divorce among military couples is high. All of us know that there are going to be hardships ranging anywhere from long separations to crummy base housing. But the one thing that I have the most trouble dealing with by far is the constant moving. Before I met Alex, I had lived in the same house, on the same street, in the same town for my entire life, and I loved it. I'm a creature of habit and order, so when you move so often that you never have a chance to create any habits, it can be a challenge, and never more so than when you are moving with kids.

I have ten children. I know it sounds crazy, and believe me, most days it is. I can't tell you the last time I had a shower or even went to the bathroom without an audience. They range in age from two to twenty, and all but two are still at home. I had my first one at eighteen and my last one at age thirty-six, and I'm *done*. After the last one, my husband jokingly said, "Brook, you know we could have a couple more; I hear they come cheaper by the dozen"

I just looked at him and said, "Honey, if you want them cheaper by the dozen, go out and buy a box of donuts. I'm through!"

He was kidding of course, and both of us love our big family. There are some people, especially in the military, who just can't understand why anyone would want this many kids, and I respect that. It's definitely not for every-body. In fact, when I first married my husband, I didn't even know that's where we were headed, but now that we're here, I wouldn't change it for the world.

There are several adjectives that come to mind when describing our family. We are military, big, happy, loving, loud, and devoted to one another. And there isn't one of those adjectives that I would describe as abnormal. That's not to say that having a big family is for everyone. It takes some important qualities that unless you possess, I wouldn't advise attempting it.

First of all, you need to have a strong constitution, because looking after a large family will wear you out faster than any job you could have outside the home. You need to be organized, efficient, patient, tolerant, and a devoted coupon clipper. You have to have a supportive husband, too, who loves kids and looks upon being with them as a gift. Otherwise, you are going to end up doing it all yourself, and everyone has their limits. Of course, when you are raising a big family in the military, chances are you will end up doing it alone anyway since frequent deployments are a way of life for most service members. But at least it helps to know that when they are home, they are going to help.

My husband was raised in a large Catholic family, so having a big family was a given for him since he looks upon his childhood with fond memories. I, on the other hand, was an only child raised by two only children, which left me with no aunts, no uncles, no cousins, and of course no brothers or sisters. I was keenly aware that everyone else had all those things while I did not. I compensated by bringing home an assorted menagerie of broken and wounded animals that my mother graciously tolerated because she knew I was lonely a lot of the time.

As our family grew, it always amazed me when we would announce that we were expecting another little Greenstone. My husband's chest would puff out with pride like this was quite an accomplishment he had managed. There he was doing what came naturally then sitting back for nine months watching me throw up, gain weight, and battle heartburn and hemorrhoids. One thing I told him from the start was, "You were there to have the fun of making this baby, so you sure as heck better be there when I go through bringing him/her into the world." I was absolutely adamant that he suffer along with me. Of course, considering the number of children we have and the amount of time Alex was deployed, I feel lucky that he was there for six out of the ten.

Actually, it wasn't quite as grisly as I make it sound. I did have some morning sickness with almost all ten of them, but it passed fairly quickly. The other annoyances usually didn't come around until the end of the pregnancy, so it was manageable.

Our first four were all girls. My husband never said he was disappointed that one of them wasn't a boy. He was just thrilled and happy that they were whole and healthy. But I couldn't help but think that he was hoping for a son to carry on the Greenstone tradition of military service.

Although he never said as much, I knew he wanted a boy, so I was relieved when number five was an Evan. Turns out, I had nothing to worry about because numbers six, seven, and eight were all boys too! By that time people were saying, "Haven't you figured out what causes this?" or "You know it's going to cost a fortune to feed all those kids and send them to college." Of course we already knew all of that, but we just went along our merry way, raising an ever-expanding family. I think people forgot sometimes, too, that with each new addition, our love was multiplied, not divided, and that this all happens gradually. You don't just suddenly wake up one morning and boom! You've got ten kids. You work into it slowly, and adding one more just never seemed to be a problem.

Having said that, however, after eight, we decided that four boys and four girls was a nice number and maybe we were through. Mother Nature had another idea, and I got pregnant again just after my thirty-sixth birthday. We had our last two, twin girls who were so identical we had to put different colored fingernail polish on their nails from birth so we could tell them apart. After the birth of the twins, we decided that we didn't want to be ridiculous about it, and since I seemed to be Fertile Myrtle, we took steps to make sure that our family was complete. We were the Greenstone dozen (including me and Alex), and our life's pattern was set.

One of the things that we enjoyed most with the birth of each new child was deciding on a name. We thought that maybe naming them alphabetically would be nice and make sense. We started with Annabelle, then Blair, followed by Candace and Danielle, then on to the boys. We added Evan, Ford, Gavin (whose delivery was so easy he practically walked out), and Harrison (whose delivery was so hard, *I* almost walked out!). Then we ended with the babies, Indiana (good thing our last name wasn't Jones) and Jasmine (Disney's *Aladdin* was the girls' favorite movie, and we made the mistake of telling the kids they could pick the names for the twins.).

Alex worked in the transportation department of the air force, and it was typical to be stationed somewhere between two and four years at a time. This wasn't always helpful though, since it seemed like every time we were in the middle of a move, I was either pregnant or managing a newborn. Moving even for a family of four is a massive undertaking. With a family as big as ours, it was nothing short of a full-scale military operation.

We had to get the medical and dental files on each one of us, and with this many kids, just keeping their shot schedules and dental checkups straight was a daunting task. We had to keep all of their birth certificates and important documents together, so we could enroll them in school. And most of the time it seemed like every school required something different, from state to state or even country to country, which made the process even more tedious.

All of this was just part of the routine of moving. In twenty-three years we have moved thirteen times, which if my math is correct is more than every two years. While every move is difficult in its own way, without a doubt it was hardest on those few occasions (three to be exact) that Alex had to be at his new duty station before we could leave. Sometimes I had to wait for the house to sell or for the kids to finish the school year. But doing all of it on my own was usually nothing short of a nightmare. Thankfully my parents were able to come and help me with each of those moves; I really don't know what I would have done otherwise.

In the life of every military wife, there usually comes a watershed moment when things become so overwhelming that they ask themselves if it's all really worth it. Common feelings might be, "This isn't what I signed up for," or "How can he expect so much of me?" or my personal favorite, "When the military starts paying me, then they can tell me what to do; until then, I've had it!" My watershed moment came during our move to Colorado.

By the time we had our sixth child (Ford), we had saved enough money to buy a beautiful house at our next destination, which was Colorado Springs, Colorado. I had never lived out west and really had no desire to. But the powers that be don't ask the wives where they would like to live when they start handing out orders. Really, I can be happy just about anywhere, but for some reason, I just wasn't looking forward to this move. The thing that helped considerably though was the house that Alex had found. For this house, I could overlook the cold winters and being so far away from my parents.

With this move, I was determined to be organized right from the start. At twelve years old, Annabelle wasn't quite old enough to be left alone to babysit the other children, and I knew I would need help getting everything together. So my mother came with us to Colorado Springs to help me get settled. She loved being around the kids, and I always cherished any time I could spend with her.

Annabelle was like a little mother hen, which turned out to be a huge blessing for me. Every time a new little Greenstone made his or her arrival, Annabelle was there to coo over and take care of the new baby. So on the long trip from Mississippi to Colorado, we took two cars with Alex in one taking Blair, Candace, and Danielle, and me and my mother in the other with Annabelle and the two youngest at the time, Evan and Ford. Blair did her best to entertain Candace (eight) and Danielle (six), and Annabelle was seated in my car between Evan and Ford. Also quietly swimming laps and waiting to join the gang was number seven. I had two months before this baby was due, and I was determined to be settled before he or she made their appearance. (We had decided from the start to be surprised at the sex of each child until they were born.)

My mother and I had packed a huge picnic lunch for our first day on the road, but we knew after that we would be stopping at restaurants. Frankly, I wasn't looking forward to it. It was enough of a challenge just coordinating everyone's bathroom stops. Candace was carsick, and just about the time she had finally fallen asleep, Danielle and Evan just *had* to stop because they couldn't hold it any longer. I was always ready to stop since I had a baby pressing down on my bladder. We had managed to leave around eight a.m. that morning, so by noon everyone was hungry. So we decided it was a good time to have our picnic.

We all piled out of the car and headed over to the picnic area. Unfortunately, people had not been careful about where they walked their pets, and it was obvious what had taken place near the picnic area. When the kids all started holding their noses and saying, "Phew, what stinks," Alex said in a loud voice, "Who ordered the poo poo platter for lunch?" The girls dissolved into fits of laughter while my mother rolled her eyes, and Alex walked over to the baby, picked him up, sniffed his behind, and said, "Wow! Ford, is that you?"

With all the indignation that a two-year-old with a limited vocabulary can muster, Ford yelled, "*I no poo poo!*" I could vouch for that since Annabelle had just checked his diaper before we stopped, but we all got a chuckle out of it, thanks to Alex. We moved on to another picnic table where the odor wasn't quite as pungent, and while my mother unpacked lunch, Alex and I took the gang to the restroom. It was a sunny day, and by the time we all returned from the bathroom, my mother had put on what we called her "horse glasses." They were a big pair of square sunglasses she wore to protect her eyes after having some cataracts removed, but they look like horse blinders.

When he first saw her put them on, Alex, ever the comedian, said, "Are you sure that your eye doctor doesn't also work as a veterinarian?" My mother was visiting us in Mississippi at the time, and I think we were all out picking blueberries. After that comment, I remember she lobbed a couple right at his head.

After everyone was watered and fed, Alex played Frisbee with the kids to help them get some excess energy out while Mom and I packed up the lunch mess. My mother took that moment of rare quiet while the kids were occupied to ask me how I really felt about this move. I responded by saying that moving always wore me out, but I knew when I married Alex that changing jobs every few years was part of the package. It's just a lot more complicated when there are children involved. Annabelle, Blair, and Candace had all left behind good friends amid a flurry of tears and promises to write. The girls had a piano teacher that they loved and a Girl Scout troop that took up a lot of their time with fun activities that would be hard to find elsewhere.

I wasn't looking forward to this move to Colorado, with the exception of where we were going to live. We had found a beautiful house with a great view of Pike's Peak, with four bedrooms and three and a half baths. I wasn't too crazy about snow. But I was usually always up for a new adventure, and moving across the country with six children would definitely qualify as an adventure.

Before we left on every trip, I would make up a travel bag for each child. It would contain their favorite snacks and juices, plus an assortment of fun-to-do activities to help keep them occupied. I found that by giving each one their own snacks, the inevitable fight over the last cookie, pretzel, orange, or whatever was avoided. Their activities varied from child to child. Annabelle and Blair liked to read, so they each got a book. Candace got sick when she read in the car, so she liked to make animal pipe cleaners and origami. Danielle was usually satisfied with paper dolls. Thankfully, these were all quiet activities.

The boys at four and two, though, would sleep a fair amount but get restless after a while being strapped in their car seats. I couldn't blame them; I was getting restless with my big tummy strapped in behind the wheel, too, and it seemed like the drive across Kansas took forever. I had never really seen tumbleweeds before, and I eventually learned not to flinch every time one blew out across the road in front of the car.

I was very glad, after three long days of traveling, to come over the hill as we came into Colorado Springs and see the beautiful sight of Pikes Peak, with snow still on the top. All I wanted to do was get to the realtor's office, pick up the keys to our house, get there, and get everyone settled in at least for the night. We had brought the basics with us, all packed in a U-Haul that Alex had been pulling behind his car. We had enough air mattresses for all of us, plus sheets, pillows, blankets, towels, and basic kitchen supplies. I figured we could make it for a couple of days until our household goods shipment arrived.

We had closed on the house while still in Mississippi, and the papers were sent overnight to Colorado. Alex had come out and found the house, taken a lot of pictures, and made our offer over the phone after he returned home to discuss it with me, so I hadn't actually seen the house yet. The pictures told me all I needed to know though, and I couldn't wait to get inside. It had been a couple of months since he had been to Colorado Springs, and I guess after the long drive and with the girls squabbling in the backseat, he was having a hard time finding the realtor's office. I followed obediently behind him as we circled the same area four times, but my patience was wearing thin. I could tell Alex was getting frustrated by the sound of his voice over the walkie talkies. My mother, bless her soul, kept saying, "It's getting late, dear. The children need to eat and get into bed." Of course, I was well aware of both these facts as one of the "tired, hungry children" had been kicking the back of my seat for the past thirty minutes.

"Whoever is kicking my seat better knock it off, or there are going to be big time outs in your future … *big* time outs! Who wants to spend the first night in our new house getting acquainted with the corner?" I yelled to the perpetrator in the back seat.

"Me!" Annabelle said. "I'll sit in the corner if it means I can get out of this car! How do we know this house even has corners?"

I replied calmly, "I trust your father, dear. The houses he finds always have corners ... and what's that stench?"

Little four-year-old Evan piped up and said, "Ford is stinky! He gots a poopey diaper!"

Then my mother said in a weak voice, "My heavens, Brook, what has the baby been eating?" fanning herself as the smell started to invade every corner of the car. I started to feel sick myself, and I radioed to Alex that unless he found this place in the next five minutes, I was bailing out to the nearest Wal-Mart to change Ford's diaper and get everybody a snack.

Annabelle said, "I'm not changing one more diaper ... not for a thousand dollars!" She had been a huge help for the entire trip, and I couldn't blame her; we were all getting to the end of our tethers.

"I'll do it," I said as Alex slammed on the brakes in front of me and finally pulled into a parking lot, which I fervently hoped was the realtor's office so we could get the key. The good news was that it was the right place. The bad news was that there wasn't a soul there. I just sat there staring at the darkened office building in disbelief. Then I looked around the car only to find that everyone (including my mother) had bailed out the minute the car stopped in an attempt to get away from poor little stinky Ford, who sat there innocent as could be, sucking on his thumb and bouncing his little legs up and down, which only succeeded in helping the smell waft through the car even faster.

I undid my seatbelt and eased myself out from behind the wheel, which at that point meant to Ford that he had been completely abandoned. He pulled out his thumb and started to howl pitifully, and as I attempted to waddle around to his side of the car, I was bombarded by Blair, Candace, and Danielle, who were all bursting to report that Daddy had said a bad word on his fourth circle around the block.

"Great! You little traitors…just sell me down the river for a dime!" he said half jokingly.

I was glad that he still had his sense of humor, but I wasn't willing to take any bets on how long it would last. He came over and rubbed my lower back as I finally made it over to Ford's side of the car. Alex reached in, unbuckled him, and immediately realized why we had all bailed out so fast. "Come here, little man, Daddy will get you cleaned up."

I smiled gratefully at my husband and looked around before I dared to ask him what we were going to do, as it appeared that the place was closed. He replied that there was an agent on duty sign in the window, and as soon as he was done with Ford, he would call and have them come and let us in to get the key. We let the kids run around in the parking lot, stretch their legs, and get some energy out while my mother fished some juice boxes out of the cooler.

After Alex called and we all waited around for twenty minutes, the duty agent appeared, and again there was good news and bad. He opened the office for us and led us to the right desk, only to find that the agent had failed to leave us the keys to our new house. I just stood there wanting to cry at that point, and Alex was on the verge of finally losing it.

"We've been driving for three days. I have my wife, my mother-in-law, six children, and one on the way. I did my part by getting here when I said I would be here. How do you purpose to make this right on your end? I called your agent this morning. She said she would be here waiting; what happened?" Alex asked firmly.

The guy was beginning to look a little nervous as we all stood there waiting for him to answer. I was sure to him we looked like a threatening mob (just by sheer numbers), and I have to admit, I could tell Alex was getting angrier by the minute. I knew my mother had one of her best "now you've done it" looks on her face. I just looked like I was about to break into tears, which if he was a typical man was enough to scare him into action. He quickly shifted the blame by saying that this particular agent had an emergency and had to leave town. He admitted that certainly she should have left the keys but in her haste may have forgotten to.

After another quick search of her desk and still no keys and no help from this obviously overwhelmed agent, my husband finally just said, "Fine, it's my house. I'll get in somehow, even if I have to break a window, but you can tell that realtor for me that she will be getting the bill for the damage."

The agent nodded and as a last attempt at civility (or because he was desperate to get rid of us) rushed to hold open the door.

At that point I knew that no matter how anxious we were to get to the house, the kids, my mother, and I needed to eat something. I wanted us to all get to the house at the same time, so I approached Alex and told him that we needed to stop and get food before we went to the house. He looked at me with a "you've got to be kidding" look on his face while he was clearly envisioning trying to control six rowdy, tired kids at a McDonald's. He nodded, didn't say anything as he got into the car, and slammed the door a little bit harder than was necessary. But I didn't blame him a bit; tonight's circumstances would have pushed anyone's limits.

Surprisingly, the kids were so tired that they were no trouble at all during dinner. We had one adult for every two children, and the baby fell asleep on Alex's shoulder after the first fifteen minutes.

Finally we arrived at our new home, and it was everything I had hoped it would be. It was a little set off and surrounded by woods on two sides, with a great view of Pike's Peak on the backside. We still had quite a bit to do just to find our way around the house and get everyone's bed pumped up and made. By then I was so tired that I was ready to sleep in the car. There were no lights on, so Alex got a flashlight and walked cautiously to the front door. He wanted to check the windows first to see if any were open by chance before he decided which one to break.

As luck would have it, the front door had been left unlocked. Apparently the agent had been out to the house earlier in the day and had left a welcome note, a large basket of fruit, and some candy for the kids. And low and behold, there on the counter were the house keys. We learned later that she had received her emergency call while she was at our house and knew she wouldn't have time to get the keys back to the office before she left town, so she just left them there. Unfortunately, she neglected to tell *us* that, but I was just relieved that Alex didn't have to break into our new house and that no one *else* had decided to break in through our open front door before we got there.

Within an hour, everyone had explored the house, Alex had pumped up the air mattresses, my mother had found sheets and sleeping bags and gotten the girls organized in one room with herself in another, and Evan and Ford were sound asleep in our room. I had managed to find everyone's pajamas, said prayers with the girls, and hugged my mother goodnight before I waddled into our master bedroom and kissed all three of my "boys." Then, after brushing my teeth, washing my face, and slipping a maternity gown over my head, I looked down at Alex, already asleep on our queen size air mattress, and wondered how in the world I was going to get myself down there. Too tired to do anything else, I got down on my hands and knees beside the mattress and just "rolled" into it. Before I knew it, I was curled up next to Alex, and baby number seven and I drifted off to sleep.

After two days, it was finally time for us to receive our shipment, and everyone's hopes were high that things would arrive and be in good condition. The truck was on time, and before we knew it, four big, burly men began unloading box after box after box. We had tried to label each room—

girls' room, boys' room, master bedroom, guestroom, and kitchen—in the hopes that the boxes might actually end up in the right place, and to a certain extent, it worked.

I was exhausted and trying to stay seated and put my feet up, so I had the job of marking off each box on the inventory sheet as it came off the truck. My mother and the girls were trying to entertain the boys and stay out of the way of the movers, and Alex was directing traffic inside the house. It began to get cold. After a while it even started spitting some snow, so I had to move inside. By the time the truck was half unloaded, the snow was coming down in earnest, and I was getting nervous.

Just as I was wondering what else might go wrong, Alex was called into work, and things went downhill from there. He had already checked in and been to his first day of work, and they had told him he could have the day off to receive his household goods shipment. But obviously something came up that was important enough for him to be called in.

I was mad that Alex had to leave and I was in charge again. I was feeling sick to my stomach, the movers were ready to take a break, and everyone was hungry. The plan had been for Alex to go out and get food for everyone, including the movers, but he wasn't there. I didn't know my way around yet and wouldn't have left my mother alone with six kids and four movers anyway. I decided the best thing to do was order pizza and hope that they would deliver in the snow.

We had a few supplies left over and some fruit from the realtor's basket, so we were able to get Evan and Ford fed. Then we put them down for a nap in the big Jacuzzi tub in the master bedroom bath. We put down a sleeping bag and a couple of blankets in the tub, and they curled up like two little peas in a pod. I had Annabelle sit with them until they fell asleep, just to be sure they didn't try to turn on the water, but they were asleep within ten minutes. I was sorely tempted to crawl in there with them, but with Alex gone, I had to keep things moving. My mother kept shaking her head saying I was doing too much, but what choice did I have?

I asked the movers to continue bringing furniture in until lunch arrived since the amount of snow falling was making me more than a little nervous. They still had to bring in our piano, my china hutch, and our antique desk, and there was already an inch of snow on the ground.

Also keeping me on edge was the strange feeling that I was getting on the left side of my face. I pushed it to the side, thinking that I was probably just tired. An hour later, as we all pulled up a box and sat down to eat the pizza, I took a drink of soda, and it dribbled out of my mouth and down onto my shirt. Something was definitely wrong.

I excused myself, went into the bathroom to look into the mirror, and was horrified to see that the left side of my face seemed to be sagging. I tried to smile, but only the right side of my mouth curved up; the left side didn't move. I knew something was happening to me, and I was suddenly afraid for the baby. I had been so busy that I hadn't noticed if it had moved recently, and I quickly laid my hands on my tummy hoping to feel the baby kick.

After a second or two, I felt a wiggle and relaxed a little, but I still had the problem of my face. Was I having a stroke? What was I going to do? Alex was gone, I wasn't even sure how to reach him, and if I told my mother what was happening, I was sure *she* would have a stroke. The girls were too young to be of any help, and it would probably just scare them. And I wasn't about to confide in four total strangers.

The tears started to flow, and I was sure this was the moving day from hell. I hadn't wanted to come to Colorado in the first place, I was weary from traveling and looking after six children, my back hurt, my feet were swollen, and now half my face seemed to be paralyzed. It was all too much, and suddenly I knew I just couldn't take any more. This was my watershed moment, and as I sat there sobbing on the toilet, I asked myself why I had ever agreed to be a military wife and subject myself to everything I had been through during this move.

Just as I was really starting to feel sorry for myself and was wondering how much an airline ticket back to Mississippi would cost, I heard a knock at the bathroom door and Alex asking me if I was all right. I was never so glad to hear my husband's voice. I opened the door, pointed to my face, and tried to smile through my tears. When only half my face cooperated, he could tell immediately that there was something wrong and said, "We need to get you to the hospital."

I shook my head no, afraid that if I spoke it would sound funny and then I would really start to panic. Alex called the Air Force Academy Hospital there in Colorado Springs and talked to a doctor about what was happening to me. The doctor asked some questions, mainly if I was having any numbness or paralysis in my arms or legs, which I wasn't. It seemed to be confined to my face, which indicated to the doctor that it was probably Bells Palsy. He said I should be checked. But right now, the snow was coming down pretty hard, and it probably wasn't worth the risk of driving unless my symptoms got worse. He told Alex that I should go to the ER if anything changed drastically and that I should come in as soon as it was possible in the morning.

I was satisfied with that, but my mother was not. Once she heard the word "palsy," she went very white and began to imagine all sorts of crippling scenarios. Alex pulled out a chair for her and said that although he wasn't trying to minimize it, he had known a guy who had gotten this before and it seemed to be something that was confined to one side of the face and would eventually go away, usually without any lasting side effects. My mother and I both said,

156 · Terry L. Rollins

"Usually?" at the same time, except that mine sounded more like "woosilly?"

Alex went immediately to the movers and asked that two of them set up our bed right away because his wife was expecting (as if they hadn't already noticed) and wasn't feeling well. Two of the men came in, stomped the snow off their boots, took their coats off, and grudgingly put our bed together. I refused to feel guilty even though I knew they were in a hurry to finish unloading the truck and get out of there before the snow got too deep. But the rules were that whatever was taken apart on the other end had to be put back together on this end. And I really did need to lie down. The bed was put together in less than ten minutes, Mother and I found the box labeled bedding, and she and Alex made the bed. Before I knew it, I was warm and cozy under a thick comforter, I had changed into my nightgown, and all I wanted to do was sleep. I had made it through my watershed moment, and I had calmed down some. But if someone right then had asked me what it was like to be a military wife, I would have told them that being married to the military was a nightmare that no sane woman should ever have to endure!

The rest of the day was not without its drama. The movers slipped coming into the house while carrying my piano and broke one of the legs. I wasn't around to tell them where to put the piano, so Alex just made an educated guess, which happened to be the complete opposite of where I had intended to put it. My mother accidentally walked into the bathroom while one of the movers was using it (who doesn't lock the bathroom door in a house with six kids in it?) and was duly traumatized. She claimed later it was responsible for at least a dozen additional grey hairs. And at one point amid all the boxes and mayhem, the girls lost Ford.

They had been playing hide and seek, and suddenly he was nowhere to be found. It was getting dark, and the movers were just finishing up and wanted Alex to sign the paperwork, when Annabelle came up to report that Ford was "missing." Alex immediately stopped what he was doing (much to the displeasure of the mover, who was anxious to get out of this madhouse) and said, "This will only take a minute." The mover (I think his name was Buford) opened his mouth to protest, and Alex said very firmly, "My two-year-old son is missing, and *no one* is going anywhere until I find him."

Now when you have as many kids as we do, occasionally one will go missing. They aren't really gone, just hiding or asleep somewhere, so Alex wasn't too worried yet. But he still wasn't taking any chances, and he quickly ordered everyone to spread out and find Ford but not to go into my room. Well, it turns out that was the first place they should have looked, because unbeknownst to me, Ford had gone looking for Mama and had pushed a box beside the bed, climbed up, and snuggled in beside me.

After a thorough search of the house and still no luck, Alex came in quietly, looked around the darkened room, and then began to pat down the comforter checking for a little lump, which he happened to find resting against my back. He pulled the cover up to find Ford, in his sweatpants, sweatshirt, only one sock on, and sucking his thumb, fast asleep. Greatly relieved that all his offspring were safe and accounted for, Alex tiptoed out of our room and told everybody that the little lost sheep had been found. My mother, who had just begun getting the "vapors" out of fear that Ford had wandered off in the dark and the snow, was so relieved she started to cry. The four girls immediately converged on "Nana" with hugs and kisses, and Evan went back to playing with his Legos.

After the movers were finally gone, Alex decided that food was the first thing to be accomplished, as all the kids had started complaining they were hungry. We had seen a chicken place about a mile from the house, so he told my mother that he was going to make a dinner run then stop by the convenience store and get some bread, cereal, milk, juice, peanut butter, and jelly, just in case it snowed all night. She nodded, said that she would try to find some paper plates and cups, and asked him to please pick up some toilet paper. She asked Annabelle and Blair to stay and help her in the kitchen, and Alex volunteered to take Candace, Danielle, and Evan with him. I, of course, was sound asleep and oblivious to all of this, but apparently Alex was able to navigate the snowy roads without any problem, and the rest of the night went very smoothly.

Everyone felt better after they ate, Alex got the beds put together (much to my mother's relief since she had rolled off of her air mattress at least twice the night before), and although he was too tired to make everyone take a bath, he did make sure everyone put on pajamas and brushed their teeth.

Just before bed, he turned off the lights in the living room and led everyone through a maze of boxes to the large window at the front of the house. It was a beautiful sight. The moon was full, the snow was still gently falling, and everything was quiet. Alex had everyone hold hands, including Nana, and they said their bedtime prayers, thanking God for another safe move and asking that Mommy feel better. Then everyone scampered off to bed, and Alex checked and locked all the doors, turned off the lights, thanked my mother for all her help, and finally, at 12:20 a.m. after a very long day, carefully got into bed with me and Ford and was asleep within five minutes.

The next morning when Alex took me to the Air Force Academy Hospital, we learned that I did in fact have Bells Palsy. It sounded scary, and I knew that when I told my mother she was going to blame it on me doing too much. But the doctor explained that it should eventually go away by itself with little to no lasting effects. I had to laugh, though, when he told me to try to cut down on my stress and get some rest.

"Doctor, I am a military wife, and I have six kids and one on the way. How do you propose that I cut down on my stress?"

He shifted his feet slightly, scratched his head, and said, "I'm not sure what the answer is to that one."

"Well, not moving again any time soon would be a start." I looked hopefully at Alex.

He helped me down off the examination table and promised to do his best.

───────────

That night after everyone was in bed, Alex and I had a long talk about the sacrifices we were both making in order for him to be in the military. I admitted to him that there were days that I felt like the kids and I came a distant second behind his career, and I didn't like it. When he asked me if I ever wished he would retire, I was honest and said yes. He seemed a little surprised.

"I knew things were hard on you sometimes, but you never complained, and everything always seems to run like clockwork. Maybe I have been taking you for granted."

We were side by side in our bed. He began to gently stroke the side of my face that was affected by the Bells Palsy, and I reached out and pressed my palm against his chest.

"Alex, you're a good man with a good heart who made the decision to serve his country because for you, it's the right thing to do. What purpose would it serve for me to deny you the opportunity to do what you were meant to do? Plus, I knew when I married you what I was getting in to. Granted, the moving has been harder on me than I thought it would be, and I certainly never expected to get something like Bells Palsy. But we have a beautiful family, and we love each other. I guess if every thirteen years I have a meltdown like I did yesterday, then we can handle that, right?"

"Absolutely" he said as he pulled me close.

The Bells Palsy got worse before it finally got better. For most of that time, I felt like the left side of my face was going to slide off my head; eating and drinking became a daily challenge as well. But the symptoms did pass eventually, and when Gavin made his appearance a little early one snowy night, it turned out to be one of my easiest deliveries. We even had his nursery all set up and ready for him.

My memories of our move to Colorado are mixed. Giving birth to Gavin and becoming pregnant with Harrison were two events during that time that enriched our family tremendously. But I will also remember it as a time when both Alex and I were forced to take a long hard look at what it really meant for us to be a military family, to honestly decide if all the sacrifices we were forced to make on a regular basis were worth it.

Tonight, many years later, I am sitting in a rocking chair holding my youngest child, one of our twins, as she sleeps peacefully in my arms. We are preparing for yet another move. But for now, all is quiet, the sun is slowly setting over the base, and I can hear the lone bugle playing taps as it does every night at this time. And as that beautiful, haunting melody brings to a close another day, I know that I am blessed. I'm blessed to be able to call myself an American, I'm grateful for my husband and my children and as I close my eyes, and I know without a doubt that this is where I'm supposed to be … married to the military.

Camille
MY DEMON WITHIN

I stood in my office looking out at the beautiful scene before me. The snow had been falling all across the metro DC area since early that morning, but this was the first time I had taken time to notice it. I gently rested my aching forehead on the cool glass and closed my eyes. My mouth was dry, and I could feel the muscles in my neck beginning to tense up as I prepared myself for the battle I knew lay ahead as soon as my workday was over. My body would be craving, demanding, that drink, and my mind would plead with me to be stronger than the beast within me. But the overwhelming physical urge to wrap my hands around that glass filled with ice and my life's poison always won in the end.

I opened my eyes to watch the snow blanket the city in a sea of white and wondered with a sense of irony what the many constituents in my congressional district would think if they really knew the twisted soul that resided in their highly thought-of congresswoman, not that I really cared that much anymore. I had long since let whatever pride I had in my job as a public servant be consumed by the demon within me, a beast that no matter how hard I tried to conquer always teamed up with my crippling self-revulsion to beat me down, time and again.

I turned to look at the picture of my grown children and their families sitting on my handsome and expensive mahogany desk and felt cold inside, the exact opposite of what I knew I should feel when gazing at my own flesh and blood. It had been a long time since I had allowed myself to feel anything where my children were concerned. It had proved to be too painful. My exile was self-imposed, or so my children told me, but they didn't realize that I knew how they really felt about me. But those discussions were never had when I did see them, which was less and less frequently as the years went by, it was a simple, if somewhat unfulfilling, experience that did little more than scratch the surface of our everyday lives. But what could I expect after all this time? How could I even begin to ask more of them than I was willing or able to give myself?

I had picked the perfect place to work and live. The fast-paced, every-man-for-himself, dog-eat-dog way of life in the nation's capital was a perfect place to hide from yourself, from your colleagues, and really, from the whole world. If you knew how to play the game, you could get through every meeting, every press conference, and every congressional session with your reputation intact and your backside out of the line of fire. It was almost comically endearing whenever the freshman congressmen and women were sworn in, all full of hope and promise, wearing their hearts on their sleeves, ready to slay the dragon that ruled with an iron fist—the machine that is American politics. I no longer wore my heart on my sleeve and most days doubted that I even had a heart at all.

Was it always like this? No, once upon a time long ago, I had a heart, a soul, a family, and a husband that I was proud of. But life is full of decisions, some hard, some easy, some you can take back, and others you only wish you could. What am I today? I am a middle-aged congresswoman, impeccably dressed, respected by my peers and constituents, and in control at all times, at least on the outside. On the inside, I am a shell of a human being, wracked every day with the burden of guilt that I carry with me and nurture every night in a bottle of vodka. And on days that I allow myself to remember, I am a military wife of a man dead long ago, dead because of me.

As I turned from the window to look at the clock, I realized that I have been daydreaming for over thirty minutes, and the snow is still thick and steady. I had already urged my staff to leave early to try and avoid the rush that was sure to plague the beltway as people begin to realize that this snowstorm is here to stay, at least for the next forty-eight hours.

My drive home was uneventful, quiet even as everything around me was blanketed in a soft, dewy layer of white. I arrived home to an empty house, beautiful on the outside but lacking warmth and life on the inside, just like its owner. I tossed my coat and gloves on the bench in the entry foyer. There were no messages, my mail was minimal, and my contact with the outside world, for the moment, was blessedly suspended.

I kicked off my shoes, walked quietly into the library where I keep my liquor cabinet, and poured myself a drink. As I swirled the ice around and allowed the feeling of holding the glass in my hand begin to soothe me, I realized that once again I am faced with a long, lonely weekend, with nothing but my booze and my memories for company. I took a long sip of my drink, which was cold but burned like fire going down, an interesting juxtaposition that never ceased to amaze me. I flicked on the propane fire in the fireplace that is the center of my library and decided to curl up in the big leather chair and relax for a few minutes before I had to think about what to do for dinner.

As I began to glance around this stately room, my gaze fell upon my favorite picture of my father, a good, hard-working man, who would have been amazed at the idea that I could start my fire at the flip of switch. Although he worked for the railroad, he wore a coat and tie every day but spent the weekends with his sleeves rolled up doing what I call "hard labor" jobs like chopping wood, clearing brush, and making real fires.

Times seemed so much simpler when I was a child, or maybe my parents just made it feel that way. But most men I knew were like my father—honest, hardworking, and ready to do the right thing for somebody else, because "that's just what you do," he would say. He never made me feel bad about any decision I ever made, including some I cringe to think about. He was there when my husband died, and even then, at the worst moment of my life, he never judged me. Everyone knew it was my fault, even my children, but he never said a word, never a word.

I forced my thoughts away from that day, knowing that those particular memories would only drive me further into the bottle. I decided to see what I had in the kitchen that I could pull together and call dinner. Throughout the week, my housekeeper, Anna, would make me dinner on those nights that I told her I would be home. She would leave me something on a warm plate with a note telling me to enjoy my evening. I had called her earlier in the day to tell her to leave since I didn't want her getting stuck because of the snow. She had several bus changes to make before she would arrive at her small apartment, and I didn't relish the idea of being snowbound with anyone this weekend.

I found a thawed steak that I could cook in the broiler and had just begun my search for a potato when my phone rang. Without giving it much thought, I picked it up, said hello, and was surprised to hear my son Nathan's voice. Nathan is the oldest of my three children, followed by Nicholas, named for his father, and Bethany, who shares my middle name. I am Camille Bethany Lindquist Cartright, Lindquist being my maiden name.

Though there are many, many things I don't like about myself, my name is not among them. I have always liked the name Camille, and Lindquist is a good Swedish name. When I married Nick, I always felt like Camille Cartright had a nice sound to it.

I had not talked to Nate in months, although his sweet wife, Victoria, had always been good about staying in touch with a letter or two a month, inevitably with pictures of my grandchildren and detailed descriptions of their various activities. I always appreciated those letters and made a mental note to write her back over the weekend. Nathan informed me that he had just arrived in town on a last-minute business trip, but his meeting had been canceled due to the weather. Apparently, so was his flight back to Chicago. There was an awkward pause where I knew I was supposed to offer for him to stay with me, but I hesitated and he noticed.

"I can try and get a hotel if you prefer, but you've got the room. We haven't seen each other for a while," he said.

"Yes, of course you can stay here," I told him, recovering from my momentary hesitation. "Can you get a taxi, or shall I come and get you?"

He was quick to respond that no, he didn't want me driving in this weather and that he could see that traffic was still moving, albeit slowly, and he would grab a taxi. He said he thought he would be there within the hour, and I told him I would get started on dinner. He hung up, apparently pleased with himself, although why he would want to spend the weekend alone with me was beyond me.

I got another steak out and put two large potatoes in the oven. I wasn't sure we had ingredients for a salad, but when I looked in the refrigerator, I was relieved to see that Anna had gone to the grocery store, bless her. I had all that I would need for the weekend, even with Nathan here. I felt a wave of tenderness toward Anna; she was the best domestic that I had ever had. She was always looking out for me and thinking ahead for what I might need. She even left a note saying that she had changed the linens in my guest rooms, just in case the storm brought in any "refugees." I paid her well, was generous when she needed a day off, and gave her a substantial Christmas bonus every year, and nights like tonight reaffirmed in my mind that she deserved it.

I really had nothing left to do to prepare for my son's arrival other than to set the table and pour myself another drink to steady my nerves. This time around, I added some orange juice to help disguise the smell of the vodka on my breath and started to set the table. I went over to my china hutch and turned on the interior light at the top so that it shone gently down on all the beautiful crystal that I had collected during my husband's career in the navy. I chose two plates from a beautiful set from Spode that Nick had liked because it was the only set we owned that had an even remotely masculine design on it.

I found myself getting a little excited. I hadn't had any of the children for dinner in a long time, especially without their spouses. I finished setting the table with the wine goblets, silverware, linen napkins, and a couple of candles. It looked nice and welcoming, I thought, and I tried to remember the last time I had entertained in this room.

I was back in the kitchen tossing the salad when I heard the doorbell and then Nathan's steps in the foyer. "Mom, I'm here," he called out.

I stood in the entry hall, looked at my oldest child, and marveled at how much more he seemed to look like his father as he got older. He was well over six feet tall, clean shaven, with a thick head of dark hair with just the slightest touch of grey in it. He had thickened through the middle a little when he hit his forties, but still remained remarkably handsome. To me, he looked like a little boy, standing there with a big grin on his face, snow in his hair and on his coat.

"Wow, it's really coming down out there. Glad I made it!" he said as he took off his coat and reached to hug me. I stepped back from him and told him I was glad he was here. I saw a familiar look flicker across his face, just for an instant, and I wondered if he had smelled the liquor on my breath. He didn't say anything. I told him he could take his bags upstairs to whichever guest room he preferred and that he had time to wash up before dinner. I had not had time to go upstairs to check on the rooms, but I knew that Anna would have left them in good shape, with a fire laid in the room I felt sure Nathan would choose. It was the most masculine of the guest rooms, with a heavy, mahogany, four-poster bed with a big down comforter, a desk with anything he might need, a beautiful view of the city, and his own bath.

Nathan took the steps two at a time, and I smiled to myself as I heard the water running upstairs. He had indeed chosen that room, which was right over the kitchen. I poured the rest of my vodka and OJ down the drain and washed the glass, wanting to avoid any unnecessary advertising.

Dinner was nice. We caught up with each other's lives. I listened intently as he talked all about the children's activities, his job, and what Victoria was up to. I marveled at how busy they all were and was thankful that my son seemed so happy with his life. His father would have been very proud of him, I was sure. I reached for my wine glass as that familiar feeling of regret washed over me.

He asked about how things were going for me here in Washington, DC. I told him all was well and that things never really changed. The nation's capital was gearing up for the next election year, which always added a lot of energy to a city that never lacked for news and excitement on a normal day. He was looking at me intently and asked if I was still happy with my job. The question took me a little by surprise. It had been so long since I had been really "happy" about much of anything that I wasn't sure just how to respond. "It's okay, I guess. I may not have the enthusiasm that I once had, but it pays the bills," I joked.

"Mom, you have plenty of money; you don't have to work so hard."

I was surprised by his serious tone and reached to take his plate into the kitchen. "I mean it, Mom; you need to take it easy, spend more time with your family."

Nathan followed me into the kitchen as I got out the cheesecake that Anna had bought from a local deli she knew I liked.

"Everyone seems to be doing fine on their own. I don't need to be a meddling mother-in-law."

"No one would ever call you that. In fact, it's really just the opposite. We hardly ever see you."

I turned to him, unsure why the topic had come up, and asked him what he was getting at. He just said that he, Nicholas, and Bethany were worried about me. I thought I knew where this was headed, and I didn't want to go there. But I didn't say anything and simply handed him his dessert plate and motioned him into the library where the fire was still going, making the room warm and cozy. I asked him if he wanted a brandy, and he shook his head no.

"You don't mind if I have one, do you?"

He shook his head no and said, "Would it really make a difference if I did?"

I replied, "Not a bit," and sat down in my big leather chair beside the fire, directly across from where Nathan sat, brandy in my hand. I knew what was coming up, and there was no way I was going to make it through this night without a drink in my hand.

"How much have you had to drink tonight, Mother?"

I told him that it wasn't much. But as I began to add it up, "Two vodkas, three glasses of wine with dinner—"

"Four," he interrupted me.

"—and now my brandy. That's not so much, is it?" I asked him, knowing full well that it was way too much. He responded as I thought he would by saying that it was too much and that I knew it. He was right of course; I did know it but didn't feel like admitting it to my son.

"What is it you want from me, Nathan? You obviously have something in mind; what is it?"

Then he said the words that I dreaded to hear by saying he wanted to talk about when his father died. I had known this was where we were headed; he had tried this before, and it resulted in me storming out of his house and into a hotel the day after Christmas one year. But he had been clever this time. The hour was late, we were apparently snowed in, and I had had way too much to drink to storm off successfully to anywhere other than my bedroom. So I decided to play his game and said, "Fine, Nathan, but I don't see what purpose it could possibly serve."

He was quick to respond by saying, "Well, I do, and it's got to be done. You have tortured yourself long enough, Mom. It's got to stop."

I reminded him that I had been all through this with that ridiculous therapist that Bethany had dragged me to after Anna had found me passed out on the floor of my bedroom on an anniversary of Nick's accident. I had resented their intrusion when they forced me to go, and I told them that I would deal with their father's death my own way.

"But you're *not* dealing with it!" Bethany had screamed at me after a long night of confrontation in my bedroom, me in my nightgown with a bandage over my eye where I had banged it on the bedpost when I passed out. I had so far managed not to embarrass myself in public, but the minute

I was alone in my house, with nothing but memories, my guilt, and my shame, I had no control over the alcohol at all—none.

I pulled my knees up tight against my chest in a futile attempt to block out the words I knew I would hear and the memories that I knew my son was going to force me to relive.

It was 1970, and we were stationed in Guam. Life on base was safe and convenient. Friendships were made quickly between wives whose husbands flew combat missions into Vietnam and their children who had the run of the base. Fun spots for the kids included a movie theater, a bowling alley, and a youth center where there was always something interesting going on to keep the kids' minds off all the planes that were constantly taking off on another mission and especially off those that never came back.

Every few weeks it seemed another base family would get the news of a plane that had gone down, and more often than not, the waiting and agonizing would begin as loved ones waited for word on the fate of the crew. So far, we had been spared. Nick and all of our friends had made their missions and returned home, and now the end was in sight. Nick had received his orders to return to duty stateside, and there was only one more week that he would be making those dangerous runs that kept me up nights worrying myself sick about him, relaxing only after I heard that he had returned safely to the aircraft carrier that was the staging platform for their missions.

We were so excited about returning home. The Fourth of July holiday was coming up, and we were going to meet my parents at their lake house in Wisconsin, where we would all enjoy a fun weekend of water sports, relaxation, fireworks, and good food. Nick was to be stationed at the Pentagon, so after that we were headed back to the nation's capital. I was just so relieved to be getting out of this tour and returning to a normal life back in the States.

I knew our country had been divided about the Vietnam conflict, and I wasn't sure of the atmosphere we would face when we got back to DC. But anything had to be better than the constant worry and heartache that shadowed every day of our time in Guam.

We had two good friends, Rett and Lauren, whom we had become quite close to during our two years in Guam. Nick and Rett had known each other for a long time, and once Lauren and I met, we became fast friends and spent a lot of time together. Our children were close in age, and our friendship with the Prestons was one of the bright spots in our time there. Rett and Lauren were scheduled to leave Guam several months after us, but they were headed to the DC area as well. We looked forward to continuing the friendship.

After dinner one night, I noticed that Lauren was not as bubbly as she normally was, and I asked her what was wrong. She said that Rett had really been feeling the strain lately, and he wasn't looking forward to his last few months before they left. She said that he was upset because he had been scheduled to take a flight on their anniversary in the coming week, and they had made plans to go away, just the two of them. She said that he had seemed especially stressed out lately, and she was worried about him. I asked her why he didn't just go see the flight surgeon and let him know how he was feeling. Lauren said that his new job back in the States was very sensitive and required a top-secret or higher clearance. He was afraid that if he complained of mental fatigue, he might not be deemed fit for his new position. I knew enough to know that if Rett did go see someone, it would be put in his record and could jeopardize his career.

Lauren went on to say that he had been looking forward to the break next week, but because one of the guys in the squadron had an ear infection and couldn't fly, he was told to take the flight. I sympathized with her, and our conversation drifted to other topics. But that night, I expressed to Nick how mad it made me that the military provides mental health services to their members and encourages them to use it, but then penalizes them if they do. Nick said that he had noticed that Rett seemed pretty uptight lately and said that maybe he should go talk to him.

I immediately said, "No, don't do that, then he will know that Lauren mentioned it to me. Maybe you could take that flight for him, and then they could go on their anniversary trip."

"Won't he know that something is up if I offer to take the flight for him?" Nick asked me.

I responded by telling him that I didn't think so because it was their anniversary. He could just offer to do it for that reason. Nick lay there scratching his chin for a second then said slowly that he hadn't planned on flying anymore before he left, but he could if I felt it was that important to Rett and Lauren. I realized that I had just asked my husband to fly again on a mission that could very well be dangerous, and I hesitated.

"Maybe you shouldn't," "We're so close to leaving, and we don't want to tempt fate."

He smiled and said he didn't believe in fate. He said that he would talk to the scheduler and offer to take the flight. He promised it would be his last to Vietnam, and as I laid my head on my pillow, I knew how happy Rett and Lauren would be. But I also had to push out of my mind the nagging feeling that we were tempting fate by Nick taking on one more mission. We had made it through and were so close to going home. Was I crazy to have even suggested it to him?

I tossed and turned all night. I found Nick already gone when I woke up and was convinced that it wasn't worth the risk and that I would tell him when he came home for lunch later in the day. Unfortunately, when Nick got home, he said that he had already volunteered for the flight and that Rett had been very grateful. He said that it felt good to do something nice for a friend. When I looked worried, he said, "This flight is no different than any other that I have taken in the last two years, so don't worry." He kissed me on the forehead and told me how sweet it was that I had been thinking of how we could help our closest friends, and that was the last time we discussed it.

A few days later when I was keeping myself busy sorting through items I wanted to take back to the States and those I wanted to give away, I shouted to Nathan to get the door when I heard the bell ring. I figured it was one of the kid's friends coming over to play since they had been running in and out all day, providing me with a good way to keep my mind off Nick and this final flight he was on—the one I had asked him to take. Rett and Lauren had left on their trip the day before, and I was taking all the kids out for pizza later in the day. But when I looked up and saw Nathan's face as he walked into the room, I knew something was wrong.

"Mom, there are some people here that want to talk to you."

He looked nervous, and some small alarm went off in my brain. The hair stood up on the back of my neck. As I walked slowly down the hall toward the front door, a terrified calm came over me. There stood two men in uniform, serious looks on their faces, and there was only one reason they could be here.

"Is there somewhere we could talk privately?" they asked me.

I nodded mutely and led them into our bedroom, which was the only room in the house that wasn't full of kids.

Nathan and a couple of the older kids stood absolutely still in the hall as they watched us walk slowly to the bedroom. It was obvious they were aware that this was not a social call and something was wrong. As I sat down on the bed, I heard some of the other kids through our bedroom window, squealing and giggling, shooting each other with water guns. An old black and white movie was on the television. I had been watching it while I sorted clothes. I turned my attention from the window and looked at the strange faces of the men who now stood in my bedroom, Nick's and my bedroom.

"Please just tell me what happened," I said in as calm a voice as I could muster.

One of the men calmly closed the door since Nathan had quietly crept down the hall to listen. The other man informed me gently that Nick's plane had gone down behind enemy lines. When I asked if he was dead, they said that they weren't sure as of yet.

One of his wingmen had seen Nick come under unexpected enemy fire. The plane had been unable to fly, and Nick had parachuted out. They were not able to locate him after he slipped through the canopy of trees. They assured me that there was a search and rescue mission on as we were speaking and that they had every hope that they would find him alive.

"But if he went down in enemy territory, how do you know that they won't get to him before you do?"

They didn't answer my question directly but assured me that everything possible was being done to bring him back alive. I suddenly heard a furious pounding on the wall outside our bedroom, and when the officer opened the door, we found Nathan slamming his fists into the wall over and over again. I moved to put my arms around him, but he wouldn't be consoled. He ran from the house sobbing, and I found myself shaking from head to toe, not believing the nightmare I was suddenly in.

Our other two children, Nicholas and Bethany, appeared in the kitchen sopping wet and asked me what was going on. The officer asked if there was anyone that he wanted me to call. I immediately thought of Rett and Lauren, but they were gone. A momentary wave of nausea and anger flashed through me as I thought of them on their romantic getaway and Nick behind enemy lines. But I pushed the thought aside and told them that no, our best friends were not here, and I would wait to call family until we knew something more.

As it turned out, something more turned into days, then weeks. Our date of departure had long since passed, and we were still in Guam, waiting for some kind of word. They were finally able to locate the place that Nick went down, and they could see that he had walked away from the spot where he had landed. But they had not been able to find him.

Every day we spent waiting was agony. At night, my tortured attempts at sleep were futile as I tried to push from my mind all the things that Nick could be going through if he had been captured. Was he dead? Was he alive and just hiding, or was he captured and in pain? The questions and possible scenarios were endless. And as the days passed, I convinced myself that not hearing was still better than being told something I didn't want to hear.

Family members had been telling us to come back to the States and wait for news there, but I couldn't bear to leave the last place I had been with Nick. Word had spread about the circumstances of Nick taking that flight for Rett, and the strain on the friendship was taking its toll. They did everything they could for the kids and me, and Rett had been tirelessly pushing for everything possible to be done to help find Nick. But every time I looked at Rett, I was reminded that it should have been him on that flight instead of Nick.

At that point in time, I could not let myself dwell on the fact that I had actually asked Nick to take this flight. It was too much for my mind to accept; it was easier just to hate Rett and Lauren. After a while, Lauren began to sense my hostility, and coupled with her sense of guilt, it became impossible to be around one another. In a few short weeks, I had lost my husband and our best friends. Our children still played together; I didn't want to deprive them of their only source of company at a time like this. But eventually it all became too much to manage on my own, and I agreed to move stateside with our children.

Leaving Guam without news of Nick was almost more than I could bear, but it had become the general consensus among the other officers in Nick's squadron that he was most likely dead or a prisoner of war. Selfishly, I hoped he was a POW. However, I knew that could mean untold suffering for him, and I couldn't allow myself to think that I had been responsible for it. I left Guam under very different circumstances than I had envisioned, and I was a shell of my former self, barely able to put one foot in front of the other and guide our children where they needed to go.

My brother and my mother met us in Hawaii, our first stop on the way home, to help me look after the children for the rest of the trip. We arrived in San Francisco, the closest point of entry when returning to the US from Hawaii, beyond exhausted, and I tried to ignore the demonstrators outside the airport carrying signs about the "American baby killers" returning from Vietnam. My brother looked like he wanted to kill somebody, and my mother tried valiantly to keep the children from noticing and reading the signs.

Apparently there was a big anti-Vietnam rally in San Francisco that weekend, and as a final insult to injury, we learned when we arrived at the hotel that Jane Fonda was staying there. She had given herself a terrible reputation by visiting with the enemy. She gave comfort and aid to the

North Vietnamese and turned her back on the POWs from her own country, causing them untold additional suffering. Regardless of her political views, I knew I could never forgive her. I told myself that if I even saw her, I would slap her face or scratch her eyes out. Luckily for everyone concerned, I didn't see her. I felt a personal sense of outrage at the way she had treated the American POWs that she had met while she was in Vietnam.

———————

Everything seemed more real to me now, and all these feelings were threatening to overwhelm me. I was so exhausted, so worried about Nick, and so furious at myself that it didn't leave me much time to be anything else, including a very attentive mother to my children.

As I sat across from my oldest son on that snowy night, I couldn't imagine why he wanted to go through so many bad memories and bring up so much heartache.

"I can't stand to see you torture yourself any longer over something that happened so long ago," Nathan said.

I looked down into my drink and let him continue.

"Why … why do you insist on punishing yourself because you suggested that he take the flight?" he demanded.

"Isn't that enough of a reason?" I snapped.

"No, it's not. Do you really think that Dad would expect you to spend the rest of your life feeling guilty to the point that you isolate yourself from your children and your grandchildren?"

"You just don't understand what it's like to carry the burden of knowing that if I hadn't asked him to take that flight, he wouldn't have suffered what he did, you would have had your father growing up, and your children would have a grandfather," I replied adamantly. "Every little league game, every ceremony, your birthdays, graduations, all of it ... he should have been there. Every moment I spent living through all that he was missing took away a small piece of me, until there just isn't much left."

"Is that why you drink so much?"

I told him that yes, after so many years of carrying around the guilt and the pain, it was the only way I could cope with it.

"But don't you see, Mother? It's such a waste. You have so much to give. It's almost like I've lost two parents instead of one."

I looked up at my son and wondered for the hundredth time if I should tell him the facts that I had always kept from the three of them, the horrible awful truth of what their father had suffered because of me, and the images that woke me up in the middle of the night, drenched with sweat and wanting to die. I decided that maybe fate had put us together on this snowy night so that I could finally tell him the truth. Maybe then he would finally understand why it was all so much to bear, even now after all these years.

It was at this point that I began to open the darkest room in my mind that I try so hard to keep closed. "Maybe it's time that I tell you exactly how your father died," I said.

Nathan responded by saying, "I know how he died in a POW camp run by the Viet Cong in the last months of the war. We never got any more information than that, did we?" he asked.

I told him that no, that wasn't the case. I had received more information.

It was five years after the POWs were released, and Nick hadn't come home. The only thing we knew was that he had been a prisoner and didn't make it out alive. This knowledge was hard enough to live with, but then one day I received a letter from a man who had been imprisoned with Nick. In this letter, the man described the terrible circumstances surrounding my husband's death in the camp. I remember reading the letter with tears streaming down my face, horrified at every word as the scenes played out before me. I had kept the letter hidden for all these years, and now, as I was about to share its contents with my son, I wondered how he would feel about me once he knew the truth. I decided that I didn't care; the truth had to come out, and now was the time.

The man in the letter identified himself as Christopher. He said that he knew Nick well and considered him to be the finest man he had ever known. He went on to describe the daily ritual of torture and beatings, all in an effort to break the men mentally, physically, and spiritually. He said that Nick had been one of the strongest among them and for that reason was often times singled out for the harshest of treatment. As he became a leader among the weakened group of men, many of whom had been there for years, some of them began to look upon Nick as an angel sent by God to help them through these last final days of a nightmare that never seemed to end.

Christopher described the awful conditions: the heat during the days and the cold at night. Hunger and thirst were a constant, as was the filth and the stench, as prisoners were not allowed to bathe. The stronger of the men tried to support the weaker ones through prayer and encouragement any way they could. They tried their best to ignore the constant barrage of propaganda that was forced upon them morning, noon, and night. All of it was in an attempt to make them believe that they had been abandoned by an uncaring United States, telling them that even their own citizens called them baby killers and didn't want them back. But it would take more than the twisted minds of the men who beat them to make them less than what they were—Americans.

Christopher said that Nick often times received an extra beating because instead of repeating the anti-American slogans they demanded of him, he would recite the Pledge of Allegiance or start singing the "Star Spangled Banner." This was not only an act of defiance to his captors but a way of instilling strength and pride in the men who could hear him. He paid dearly for it though, and more than once was thrown into his cell having been beaten so badly he couldn't even stand.

I had been staring into the fire as I related all of this to Nathan, and as I paused to look at him, I could see that he had paled somewhat. But he was deep in thought and listening closely, so I continued. The letter went on to describe my husband's last day on this earth, and at this point, I turned away from the fire, unable to look at it as I finished the story of his life.

On that particular day, the men had all been taken (some unable to walk had been dragged) out to the central courtyard where they were told that because it was the guard commander's birthday, one of them was to die as a gift to him. This declaration filled the men with an equal amount of fear and rage as they wondered who would be chosen.

When one of the youngest and weakest among them, a young man named Adam, was called to the front, several of the officers cried out in protest. Christopher remembered that the Vietnamese officer in charge smiled a chilling smile, and he noticed that the man had yellow, crooked, and broken teeth as he said in broken English, "Then who will take his place?"

Silence fell among the group. Two officers stepped forward, Nick and another man. Nick motioned to the other officer, a man named Andrew, to come with him to pick their fellow prisoner up. Adam had tried to stand tall but in his weakened state had fallen at his tormentor's feet. Nick and Andrew carefully carried Adam back to his place among the men. Christopher said that Nick spoke quietly to him for a minute in words only he could hear and then slowly turned and took his place in front of the Vietnamese officer.

I remember that when I first read the letter, my eyes were so full of tears and my hands shaking so badly at this point that I could hardly make out the words that came next—those horrifying, terrible words.

They tied Nick's hands behind him and told him to kneel. Christopher said that Nick bowed his head, and he assumed that he was praying. No one was prepared for what happened next. Nick was quickly doused with gasoline, and before anyone could do anything to help him, he was set on fire. Several of the prisoners, including Andrew, who had also volunteered to take Adam's place, tried to break free and get to Nick, but they were held back by a line of grinning Vietnamese soldiers who obviously took great pleasure in the extraordinary pain suffered by those watching Nick die in such a horrific way.

Christopher apologized profusely that he had to be the bearer of such awful news, but he felt that people and, most of all, Nick's family should know that he died a very brave and noble death that had a profound effect on every American prisoner at that compound. It wasn't just how Nick had died that they chose to remember, but more how he had lived during his time at the camp. He stated again that we should all be so proud of Nick and that he was the essence of what it means to be an American soldier—willing to believe in principles worth dying for and putting honor before self. I told Nathan that the letter ended with a Bible verse that said, "Greater love hath no man than this, that a man lay down his life for his friends" (John 15:13, KJV).

I looked up at Nathan and saw he had tears running down his face, his head tipped back against the back of the chair, his eyes closed. We sat there, not saying a word for several minutes. Finally Nathan spoke. "Why didn't you ever tell us this, Mom?"

I told him that I didn't know; it was almost more than I could stand to read it, and I didn't want his lasting images of his father to be so brutal and horrific.

I was crying as I had so many times before. The days following the receipt of the letter were a blur of unbearable fog and pain. The guilt threatened to overwhelm me at every turn. Then came the nightmares. As I described to Nathan blurry, searing images of his father's death that haunted me for many years to come, I thought that I could see a look of understanding pass over his face.

"I know that I can't make excuses for my drinking, Nate, but I just can't let go of the guilt. I've tried … I just don't know how," I said, trembling uncontrollably.

Nathan moved across the room and bent down in front of me. "Do you really think that Dad would have wanted you to continue to torture yourself like this, year after year, isolating yourself from your children and your grandchildren?" he asked me gently. "You've got to deal with this once and for all, Mom. It wasn't your fault."

"Of course it was!" I cried out. "I asked him to take that flight for friends of ours, so they could enjoy their anniversary. If I hadn't, he would be here today! And I just can't bear it! I can't!" I sobbed.

My oldest son, still kneeling before me, wrapped his arms around me, and I laid my head upon his shoulder and cried as I hadn't in years. "I'm so sorry, Nathan … so, so sorry," I sobbed. He held me close and comforted me in a way that no one had in a long time. For years I hadn't let anyone in because I was so consumed with the burden of my guilt.

After several minutes of gut-wrenching tears, Nathan pulled me back, looked into my eyes, and said, "Mom, listen to me. No one blames you; you have to believe me. No one blames you but yourself—no one. Dad could have just as easily been scheduled for that flight. If Rett had asked him, you know he would have gone. It sickens me what they did to Dad, but we have to focus not on what *they* did, but what *he* did. I couldn't be more proud of the way he handled himself. Just think of the difference he made to the men in that camp, how strong and brave he was right up to the end. He refused to let them break him. He endured it all, Mom, with strength and dignity. Can't you do the same, for him, for us, and for yourself most of all?" he pleaded.

"God put Dad in that place in that time for a reason. We have to believe that it was all part of his plan. Otherwise it will continue to tear you apart. You've got to rise above it, Mom. Promise me you will seek the help you need to get through this."

I leaned my head back, my eyes closed and swollen from the crying, and asked myself for the first time if maybe it *was* possible to free myself from the unbearable burden that I had carried for so long that it was a part of me. Could I really ever let it go? Could I face what happened to Nick all those years ago and look upon it as anything other than my fault? In those moments, I didn't know the answer. What I did know on that cold, snowy night, alone with my son, was that I was weary of my life, weary of my constant struggle with alcohol and the unending days of pretending to enjoy a life that was in reality nothing but a shell.

Something changed on that night. After telling my son for the first time of the horror of his father's death, I felt a sense of freedom. Just saying it out loud made it seem all at once horrible but less of the monster I had allowed it to become all these years. I looked into the eyes of my son, the one who should have resented me for my role in his father's death but instead gazed upon me with nothing but sympathy and concern. In those moments I felt weak but knew that the time had come for me to be strong. I promised my son that I would seek help and would do my best to try to forgive myself. If he could forgive me, then surely with God's help, I could learn to forgive myself.

Lucy
WHAT CAN YOU DO
WITH A GENERAL?

In one of my favorite movies, *White Christmas*, Bing Crosby sings these words: "What can you do with a general when he stops being a general?" He is singing this song to an entire battalion of men who fought under a general during World War II, who after retiring wanders around a deserted inn he has purchased wondering what has happened to his life. It's an endearing, sentimental film with a couple hundred men coming back to show the old guy that they still remember him and what's more, they still respect him. By the end, Dean Jagger, who plays the general, has been touched by their efforts, his pride is restored, his inn is full of guests, and it even starts to snow! Oh, if only real life could be that sweet and easy.

My name is Lucy, and I am the wife of a retired two-star general. The military life has been good to us. It hasn't always been easy; we've moved more times than I can remember, we've had too many periods of separation to count, and my poor mother has had to scratch out our address in her address book so many times it's a wonder the poor dear didn't give up trying to keep track of us altogether! But when you're a proud American and your husband's life is based on helping to keep everything that is right about our country stay right and safe, you count yourself lucky... most of the time.

The problem with having a general for a husband is that they are usually in such a position of power and authority that they get used to everyone around them listening to every word they say (or at least pretending to), always receiving the answer to whatever question they ask, and everyone addressing them as "sir" before and after every sentence. Some flag officers (generals and admirals) become intoxicated with the heady feeling of everyone in a room standing up the minute they walk in and with the fact that there is always some underling there waiting to do their slightest bidding. This is all good and well in the workplace. Rank and order have their place, and it makes sense. It's a time-honored tradition, and I'm not complaining seeing as some of that "privilege" spills over onto the wives. Of course, if you are a wife and you try to abuse it and "wear your husband's rank," more times than not it will backfire on you.

No one minds if the general's wife uses the parking spot marked "Flag Officers Only" at the commissary (the base grocery store) because they figure she has earned that right. They will mind, though, if the general's wife walks into the base beauty salon and expects immediate service ahead of the other customers. In a small way, it's like being married to the president. You aren't the one making decisions, but you are the one that has the attention and ear of the president and the one who goes to bed with him at night. So there is an automatic but subtle transfer of authority just because of who you are married to.

In reality, the moment they come home, they are just your husband, same as always. You still have to smell their breath in the morning, clean their dirty socks, and fold their underwear, regardless of how many times they were saluted that day or how many speeches they gave or important decisions they made. The problems occur when you have to start reminding them that they are just your husband when they come home and that they need to leave their rank and title at work.

Very few flag officers' wives that I know would tolerate their husbands coming home and treating them like underlings. We were visiting with friends one evening when after dinner the admiral announced to his wife that he would like some coffee, clearly expecting her to jump up and get it. Without missing a beat, his wife replied, "Go ahead, Skippy. It's in the kitchen." He got the point.

It should be understood, however, that there are certain expectations that come with being the wife of a flag officer. Some embrace the responsibilities; others are of the opinion "It's his job, not mine ... until they are willing to pay me, I'm not doing a thing." I enjoyed entertaining and opening my home to the people who worked for my husband. The numerous receptions and parties could get tiresome, but I always knew that Bill appreciated my efforts, and luckily for me, he never hesitated to let me know that he noticed.

In all my years as a military wife, I never really took the time to contemplate what our lives would be like when my husband retired. We were just busy living our lives, one day at a time, trying to manage everything that came our way. We had our share of good and bad, just like everybody else. Many times I felt like a single parent, trying to keep our two children in line. Billy was always willing to discipline them when he was home; the problem was that he wasn't home that much.

As the kids grew older, it became increasingly difficult for them to "take orders" from their dad. Billy was always in a position of leadership and responsibility throughout his career, and I think that he automatically expected he would find the same kind of organization and respect at home that he enjoyed at work. Unfortunately, that wasn't always the case. Of course the kids loved their dad, but when you miss so many dance recitals and ball games, you kind of lose your right to have a say about their everyday lives, or at least that was the kids' argument.

We had our share of shouting matches between my husband and our son, and tears of frustration from our daughter when Dad came home and was "totally unreasonable." Of course everyone expected me to be on *their* side. I tried not to take anyone's side, but you know how that goes... easier said than done. But we made it through those difficult teen years, and before we knew it, both kids were off at college. The house was suddenly very quiet, and we both began to start thinking about the real possibility of retirement.

By this time in our lives, Bill had enjoyed a long and successful career. I had gone along for the ride and had raised our children, made some wonderful friends, and had memories I knew would last me a lifetime. But it was time to move on to the next stage of our lives.

With Bill's current job nearing an end, we began to think about what exactly we wanted for his retirement ceremony, a time honored tradition in the military. This ceremony was an opportunity for us to reflect back on all Bill's years of service and to thank all the many people who had made an impact on our lives along the way. We sat down together to come up with a guest list and very quickly realized that we had been blessed with many, many friends over the years. I think in all the excitement and planning of the ceremony, we never had a chance to think about what being retired really means

Our children, Emily and Ben, put together a beautiful montage of pictures of Billy's entire army career on CD, from start to finish with the appropriate music, and it was quite moving when it was played before the crowd of over 250 people who came to wish him well. There were speeches, plaques, awards, handshakes, flowers for Emily and me, and a heartfelt thank you and good-bye from my husband that had us all teary-eyed by the end. I received a beautiful quilt made by wives from the group, and I was very touched at the care and detail that had obviously gone into getting something like that accomplished. After an hour and forty-five minutes of ceremony, the cake was cut, Billy and I were toasted, and it was over. It was a lovely ending to a wonderful career, and before we knew it, we were in a long receiving line shaking hands with people from the past and the present, all wishing us happiness for our future.

The gifts, plaques, and various pieces of memorabilia were boxed up by Billy's aides and were to be mailed to our new home in Asheville, North Carolina. As we left the base after the ceremony, I was looking ahead to our new life in the beautiful Blue Ridge Mountains. As I glanced over at Bill and noted the suddenly pensive look on his face, I wondered if he was as excited about leaving all this behind as I was. I figured we would have plenty of time talk about that later, but for now we were off on a two-week cruise with Emily and Ben and some close family friends before we settled down for good. The cruise was a whirlwind, and we had a great time. We had a couple of rocky days, and Emily and I got a little seasick. However, it was a trip that we would all remember for a long time.

When we finally arrived in Asheville, I just wanted to get settled in our new house—our forever house. We had moved around so much that I still couldn't get used to the idea that this was our last home and it was really ours. We weren't renting, we weren't going to sell it, and I could paint, decorate, and do whatever I wanted to with it. It was going to be great, and I couldn't wait.

We had spent the last ten days before Billy's retirement ceremony in a nice hotel near the base. My sister and I had already flown to North Carolina before the ceremony to receive the movers at our new house in Asheville, and the furniture was all in place. But when we got home from the cruise, we still had a lot of unpacking, organizing, and decorating to do.

The first night we were home, it felt almost like when we were first married. In fact, Billy jokingly said he would like to carry me over the threshold of our new house, but he didn't know whose back it would hurt worse, his or mine. We had been pretty healthy over the years, but the ravages of age were starting to creep up on us. Neither one of us was as spry as we used to be. When we snuggled into our bed that night, I was looking forward to sleeping in and having a leisurely day around the house. I guess I should have mentioned this to my husband. I just assumed that he would want to sleep in, too, but apparently his internal clock was still set on military time.

It was Monday morning, and by 8:00 a.m. Billy had already been up for over an hour, worked out, had breakfast, read the paper, and made a list of priorities to accomplish for the day. I, on the other hand, was still sound asleep, head deep into my pillow, when I felt Bill tapping me on the shoulder saying softly, "Come on, honey, it's time to get up."

He had to be kidding! I rolled over, opened one eye, and told him I had planned on sleeping in this morning.

"You did sleep in; it's already 8:00!" Bill said. Not wanting to hurt his feelings, I said okay, slowly sat myself up, and reached for my robe. Billy looked at me cautiously and said, "How late do you usually sleep on the weekdays?"

I rubbed my face and said, "I don't know, honey; it depends on what I have going on. Why?"

He answered with the enthusiasm of a kid with a new toy and proudly waved the list in my face of all that we had to get done today.

I flopped back on to the bed and said in a weary voice, "Bill, you may not be aware of this since for all these years you have left the house at the crack of dawn every morning, but I am not a morning person. It takes me a while to get going, and I have my own little routine in the mornings."

His response left me groaning. "Well, we will have to work on all that. But for now we have a lot to get done today, so up, up, up!"

I stumbled into the bathroom, washed my face, brushed my teeth, put my hair up in a ponytail, and made my way into the kitchen, where my husband was standing at the stove with an apron on cooking eggs. Before I knew it, he had placed a steaming cup of coffee in front of me (I usually drank tea), two eggs scrambled with salsa on the top (somehow the idea of eggs and onions just wasn't sounding appealing), and a sugary donut that must have had at least 500 calories in it (I usually had an English muffin with a little butter and jam). Although I appreciated the effort and somehow managed to choke it all down, I realized that we were going to have to get to know each other's daily habits and routines again. I hadn't been alone with my husband, all day, every day for ... well, *never* actually.

As the day wore on, I realized that he and I did not necessarily have the same idea about what "retirement" meant. I wanted to take things slow and savor the moments of setting up the house, and Billy saw it as a job to be done with speed and efficiency. We were in trouble. I had heard stories from other wives who said that their husbands drove them nuts after they retired. I listened and laughed along with everyone else, but I never thought it would happen to us.

Suddenly, Billy was everywhere. When I left the room, he'd ask where I was going; when I picked up the phone, he'd say, "Who are you calling?" I couldn't tell if he was being controlling or just curious, but he was driving me crazy. I had never had someone on top of me 24/7 like this. It was going to take some getting used to.

In the course of the next week, he organized the garage (every rake, shovel, and hoe had its own place); made three matching bins for our recyclables; wrote out a schedule for the dog's heartworm pills and shots, which he posted on the refrigerator; organized the last ten years worth of tax returns; built a doghouse for a dog that only goes outside when she has to do her "business"; wrote at least two responses to the editor of the local newspaper about the best way the town could track down deadbeat voters; had the tires rotated on both our cars; balanced my checkbook; and organized my spice rack...alphabetically! And this was just in the first week. I was never going to make it. Something had to be done.

On the first day of the second week, when he approached me with a diagram to landscape the entire backyard of our new house by himself (I can count on both hands the number of times he had even cut the grass in all our houses combined), I felt like I had to talk to him.

"Bill, dear, why are you so intent on staying busy every second? I thought retirement was supposed to be a time for you to finally relax, play some golf, lie in the hammock, read a book, and take walks. You are working way too hard. What's up?"

He just looked at me and shrugged his shoulders.

"I don't know. I just feel like I ought to be *doing* something with my time,"

I told him that I agreed but that he should slow it down a notch. He did try to relax a little bit more, but it just didn't suit his nature to be idle. For me it was just the opposite. I was thrilled with all the time I had to do basically whatever I wanted to. For Bill, by the end of the month, the bloom was off the rose, and he was beginning to feel like this retirement deal wasn't all it was cracked up to be. One afternoon after he had gone to the grocery store to get a few items for me for dinner, he walked in, slammed the door, dropped the grocery bag unceremoniously on the kitchen counter, and marched right into the living room. I found him with his arms folded across his chest staring out at the beautiful view of the rolling mountains of western North Carolina, which was one of the reasons we had chosen this lot and this house.

"What's wrong, Billy?" I asked him as I rubbed my hand up and down on his back.

"Oh, some little snot-nosed punk at the Food Lion just stole my parking spot, got out of the car, yelled, 'You snooze, you lose, dog,' and flipped me the bird! I wanted to jump out of my car, grab him up by the scruff of the neck, throw him on the ground, and make him do about 500 push ups!" he said with more than a little disgust in his voice.

I bit my lip and tried not to smile, but when I looked at Bill's face, I could tell this episode had really bothered him. When I asked him what he was thinking, he didn't answer me for a minute, but was just gazing out at the peaceful scene outside our window.

"I don't know, Luce…this has been a harder change for me than I thought it would be. Six weeks ago, I was responsible for over six thousand men and women, I made decisions every day that affected the lives of more people than live in this entire town, and today my biggest job was to make sure that I got the right brand name of a spice that you needed for dinner. In the short span of a little over a month, I have gone from having people call me 'sir' and saluting me to calling me 'hey, mister' and giving me the finger! It's a lot to take in, and I've never been that good at change anyway."

I understood how he was feeling, and I was glad that he was able to identify what was bothering him.

"It's a huge transition to make, Bill. You just have to give yourself some more time,"

"Yes, you're right. I guess it was just my ego getting bruised. I'll get over it," he replied. He put his arm around my shoulders.

The next couple of months we stayed pretty busy just working around the house. Both Emily and Ben had come for a visit, which was a nice distraction, and Billy enjoyed hearing all about their lives at school. One was at Vanderbilt, the other was at Clemson, and we hadn't had a good visit with them since the cruise. I was hoping their visit would cheer Billy up; he hadn't seemed like himself for a while now. He was always pleasant and we enjoyed our time together, but somehow it seemed like his heart just wasn't in it.

The night after Emily left to go back to school when we were lying in our bed, I told him that I was concerned about him and asked him what he thought we needed to do to get him back on track. He said that he wasn't sure what he needed but that he was just feeling like his life had no purpose to it. He said that he needed to be doing something constructive, something that would make him want to get up in the morning. I was tempted to say, "Aren't I enough?" but I knew that wasn't the problem. He had gone from having a purpose-driven, productive life to one of simple choices and leisure, and it just didn't suit him.

But what could we do? He didn't want to work. Once you've been at the top, it's hard to start at the bottom again, and I couldn't see Billy taking orders from anybody else at this stage in his life. Money wasn't a problem; we had saved and invested over the years, and while I wouldn't consider us wealthy, with Billy's ample retirement we had more than enough to suit our needs. We could travel more, which we always enjoyed, but it wasn't a permanent solution to the problem. As I tossed and turned that night, unable to find an answer, I had no idea that an answer was about to find us.

Two days later, we were out for a drive to look at the fall foliage. The brilliant shades of brown, gold, orange, and yellow filled the mountains of the Blue Ridge, and fall was a sight to behold. On our way back, just a block from home, a couple about our age was out walking their dog. Just as we started to pass them, the black, fluffy little thing broke loose from its lead and ran out right in front of our car. Billy slammed on the brakes, and thankfully, we missed the puppy by inches. I was mortified, and of course, we got out of the car to make sure the puppy was okay and to introduce ourselves. Apparently the man was retired military, and as he stuck out his hand to shake Billy's, he said, "Well, do I have the pleasure of meeting an admiral or a general?"

"Major General Bill Baxter," my husband replied as he shook the man's hand.

I was momentarily surprised that he knew Billy was a flag officer, before I realized that of course, we have a military sticker on our windshield, alongside two stars. After introductions were made and we petted their little pooch, we invited them back to our house for coffee.

They turned out to be a very interesting couple. He was in fact ex-military with a long career, and he and Bill got along like they had been friends for years. His name was Damon, his wife's name was Katie, and I found that I enjoyed my time chatting with her about their various travels, their family, and their life in the Asheville area. It turns out that they lived here only part time and spent the rest of their time during the winter months down in Florida. We had quite a few things in common, and even their puppy got along with our dog, Sunny, who is notoriously picky about the company she keeps. By the end of our visit, Bill was in high spirits, and we had made plans to get together with them again for Sunday brunch at their house.

Apparently, it had done Billy some good to be able to talk about his career and recent retirement with a fellow military man who understood the language and could appreciate the uniqueness of his situation. But far and away the best thing to come out of our chance encounter, besides making new friends, was that Damon asked Billy to come with him to visit some of the patients at the veterans' hospital in Asheville. They set the date for Saturday, and Damon was there to pick Billy up, right on time. I was anxious for them to get back so that I could hear all about it, but I wasn't prepared for the remarkable effect this trip to the VA hospital had on my husband.

I sat in stunned silence as Bill described in great detail what a moving experience it had been. It was the first time in months that he had been among a group of military men, but this was a far different experience than what he had been accustomed to. These men were weak, sick, some bruised and broken from battle, others long forgotten by family and friends. As Bill made his way around the hospital, shaking hands and listening to stories of bravery, loss, and sacrifice, he was moved as he had never been before. He had tears in his eyes when he told me of a ninety-five-year-old veteran of World War II, a small, slight man who had tried to rise out of his wheelchair as a sign of respect when he was told that Bill was a general.

He told me about a young man who had been injured in Iraq and whose fiancé had left him when she learned he was permanently disabled. The young man who had sacrificed so much for his country had never shaken hands with a general before and had certainly never had one sit and listen to him talk about his life like Bill did.

As I sat and listened to my husband talk, I saw a light in his eyes and an enthusiasm that had been absent since his retirement. He had found his purpose. It was to visit these men in the veterans' hospital who had given so much for their country but were so often forgotten after coming home. Here he had a chance to make a difference, a real difference. He could touch the lives of men that he understood and respected, and they in turn reminded him that his life could still have meaning and purpose. Suddenly retired life was much better for the both of us. I was able to stop worrying about my husband's difficulty adjusting to this new lifestyle, and Bill had a new reason to get up in the mornings.

Week after week, he began to understand that holding the hand of one lonely veteran as he left this world behind was just as important an act as any he had made while he was on active duty. He had replaced the pomp and circumstance of commanding thousands with the heartfelt task of making a difference, one person at a time, and he was a better man for it. And the people he touched were better for having known him.

If my husband was looking for a purpose-driven life as a retired general, I don't think he could have found a better one, and I'm sure the patients at the veterans' hospital would agree.

Suzanna
SEPTEMBER 11, 2001

September 11, 2001, was a beautiful day in sunny Florida. It was also a beautiful, sunny day in New York, Washington DC, and a quiet field in Pennsylvania. But on that day, a great darkness broke through the beauty of that morning—a darkness that went to the soul of people the world over. Lives were lost, dreams were shattered, and a fear unlike anything we had ever experienced before clung to the hearts of men, women, and children for many, many mornings to come.

Like most other Americans, September 11 is a day that I won't forget in this lifetime. The reasons go beyond the horror of that day, played out live on our televisions before an unbelieving world. Every person lived through that terrible day in their own way, and they each have their own memories. For me, it's a memory of a day filled with loss. During the course of this one day, I lost my sense of security, my sense that being Americans somehow made us invincible, and my faith in humanity while I witnessed the cruelty that humans can inflict on one another. My children lost their innocence as they watched people jump to their deaths rather than burn alive. I lost the feeling that I could protect them. And as that very long day unfolded, I was sure I had lost my husband, only to find that he had been spared, but my beloved grandfather had passed away, leaving me sad, grateful, fearful, and relieved all in the span of an hour. My life, like so many others, was changed forever on that day.

Florida is not my favorite place to live, but somehow, we ended up there for about a third of my husband's military career. Living in a town or a state that you have no desire to ever live in is just part of the job description of being a military wife. I was born in Illinois. I love snow and cold weather, turtleneck sweaters, hot chocolate, and a warm fire. None of these things are compatible with a life in Florida. I didn't really like the beach; every time we went, sand got into everything—our clothes, the kids' hair, their food, and of course in our car. On really hot, humid days, I felt like I was living in an oven, and it took effort just to draw breath. We tried fishing, and my son got a fishhook caught in his hand after a wild cast made by his sister. So we gave up on that idea. Then after we got the kids their first dog, it got loose one day and was eaten by an alligator that lived in a retention pond near our house. Also during the course of our time there, we had to evacuate for hurricanes three different times, all without my husband, and once in the middle of the night.

So when my husband told me that he had been assigned to the central command at MacDill Air Force Base in Tampa, I was less than excited. But this time around, I was going to put my foot down. We were going to have a house with a pool (no more beach trips) and a fireplace so I could turn the temperature on the thermostat way down and at least pretend like it wasn't crazy to have a fire in the fireplace. It also helped that my parents had moved from Jacksonville down to the Tarpon Springs area, which meant that for the first time ever, we would be living in the same town. My grandfather, whom I had always been very close to, had recently moved in with my parents after my grandmother had passed away. I was looking forward to the time I would have with him too.

So on that beautiful morning in September after I had dropped both my children off, one at the middle school and one at the high school, I was beginning to think that maybe this tour in Florida might be different. I was on the way to spend the day with my mother and my grandfather, the sky was a brilliant blue, and there was a nice, gentle breeze. All was right with my world.

Then the cell phone rang, and it was my mother. She asked where I was, and I told her that I had just dropped the kids off and was headed to her house like we had planned. She told me that she had been watching the news and a plane had just hit one of the Twin Towers of the World Trade Center in New York.

"You're kidding ... how weird," was my response. "Was it a big plane or a small one?"

She said she wasn't sure, but from the looks of it, she thought it might be an airliner. I asked her if the weather was bad in New York, and she said no, that the coverage was live and it was a beautiful day, just like in Florida. I thought of how sad it was if it was an airliner full of people, and I wondered how something like that could happen on a clear day. I told my mom that I would be right there, and we hung up.

My husband, Porter, who was a colonel in the air force, was out of town on business, but I tried to call him on his cell phone anyway. I knew that he had several meetings with various people at the Pentagon that day, and I wondered if he had heard what had happened in New York. I couldn't reach him, though, and I wasn't really surprised since I knew it was his habit to turn his cell phone off during meetings.

I also knew that there were certain areas of the Pentagon where you weren't even allowed to have your cell phone with you. So I figured I would get to my parents' house, watch FOX or CNN, and see if I could get some more information to pass along to him when I could catch him between meetings. I had no way of knowing that those few moments of peace and quiet in the car before I arrived at my parents' house would be the last I would have for days. I also had no way of knowing that by the end of that awful day, the way we look at life would be changed forever.

When I walked into the house, I found my mother just standing in the middle of their living room with a dish towel in her hands, completely mesmerized by what she was seeing on the television. I sat down on the couch and listened and watched in disbelief as the smoke poured from the north tower. I tried not to think about the people who had been on the plane or the people who had been working in the tower in the area that was hit who were surely dead. I didn't even realize that I still had my car keys clutched in my hand because I was so mesmerized by the horrific scene that was unfolding live, right before our eyes. Just as I was about to ask my mother what she knew about it so far, another plane flew directly into the second tower.

My mother let out an involuntary cry of disbelief, and I jumped up and yelled, "They're doing this on purpose. Somebody is doing this on purpose! This was planned!"

Her immediate response was "Oh, no, Suzanna, it couldn't be ... how could it be?"

I told her that I didn't know, but it was inconceivable to me that this wasn't planned out by someone. I absolutely couldn't believe they had really done it. Somebody had flown two commercial airliners into the Twin Towers of the World Trade Center. It was beyond belief, and if I hadn't seen it with my own eyes, I never would have believed it could happen. But there it was, and there I was, standing in my mother's living room watching the nightmare unfold.

My mother finally sat down, all thoughts of the morning breakfast dishes abandoned, and shook her head slowly from side to side saying, "Suzanna, this is awful, just awful."

I nodded in agreement and sat down beside her in silence as we watched pieces of the buildings come crashing down to the streets so far below. I realized after a while that what we were seeing falling from the windows was not debris but people jumping to escape the flames behind them. I couldn't begin to fathom the depth of terror they must have been feeling to know that jumping to their deaths was their only option.

My mother turned to me and asked if Porter was in New York, and I shook my head and said that no, he was in Washington DC at the Pentagon. I wondered again if I should try and call him, but realized that the news of an event of this magnitude would stop short any meetings that Porter might be in and that he would probably call me when he could.

I asked if my grandfather had the news on in his bedroom. He was ninety-three years old and dying of prostate cancer and kidney failure after a long and happy life as a military doctor and avid baseball fan. He was comfortable in a hospital bed in the master bedroom of my parents' house and was tenderly cared for by my mother and the people from hospice who came to check on him and make sure he was as comfortable as possible. She replied that no, he had been sleeping when the first plane hit, and she had gone in and turned the channel to the Animal Planet, one of my grandfather's favorites. She didn't want to distress him with the news if he woke up. I volunteered to go check on him, and she thanked me and said that she was going to call my dad at his office and make sure he knew what was happening.

I walked into my grandfather's room and saw that he was resting comfortably. He looked very old and frail, but he had a fresh hospital gown on, his hair was combed, and even in his sleep he had a slight smile on his face. I was glad that he didn't know what was happening, and I thought for just a moment how much the world had changed just in his lifetime. He had fought during World War II and come face to face with the horrors of Hitler's evil regime. Both he and my grandmother had lived through the hardships of the Great Depression. But I knew that he would be shocked if he could see what was happening in New York City in those moments. I squeezed his hand, and he stirred slightly, smiled at me, and then drifted back to sleep.

When I returned to the living room, my mother said that my father was watching the news from the office and that he would be in touch with us throughout the day. I went to the refrigerator to get some juice, when my mother said, "That's odd. It says on the scroll running along the bottom of the screen that a fire has been reported at the Pentagon."

I walked over to the television and watched the scroll, and in those moments, it felt like time stood still, not only because I knew that Porter was at the Pentagon, but because I realized that a fire at the Pentagon, right now, so close after the disasters in New York, was too much of a coincidence and that the Pentagon had probably been hit in some way too.

"Heaven help us," I said in a choked voice, "we are under attack. They must be using planes or bombs or something in an organized attack. This can't be happening ... "

Not long thereafter, it was reported that a third plane had flown directly into the Pentagon, and the nation had gone into emergency alert as the incredible, horrifying reality became clear that the United States was the object of an organized terrorist attack on its homeland. Military bases everywhere went on lock down. The president was informed of the attack and flown to safety, and the vice president and speaker of the house were whisked into hiding as everyone began to wonder how many more planes would be hijacked and where they would go. For the first time in our history, fighter jets were scrambled to fly combat air patrol over the White House. The secretary of transportation called for an immediate grounding of all commercial aircrafts flying in, around, to, or from the United States. As long as I live, I will never forget the feeling of helplessness as my mother and I stood together holding hands, watching those towers of strength and icons of the New York skyline collapse into massive piles of dust, debris, and death. We knew in those moments that people were dying, lives were being shattered, and the city of New York, the United States, and indeed the world would never be the same.

I immediately rushed to call Porter again, growing ever more anxious to hear his voice, especially now that something was happening at the Pentagon. I could feel the tension and fear begin to build up as I paced back and forth waiting for more information on what was happening in Washington, DC.

———————

My mind went back to the days in early 1990 when Porter was a part of the offensive during Desert Storm. The children were young, and we were living overseas on a military base in England. All I wanted to do was watch the television as the invasion was played out live on the air. Every thought was for Porter and his safety. The wives on base were all doing the best we could, terrified for our husbands, waiting for any kind of news and praying for the best. My husband's squadron was responsible for search and rescue, which we all understood could take them behind enemy lines. I knew how important Porter's job was. But that didn't make it any easier to see all the tracers aimed at the dark skies over Kuwait, wondering if it was my husband they were shooting at.

The men were all based far away from England. Phone calls home were difficult and didn't occur very often. I was never sure whether hearing my husband's voice made me feel better or worse. I was relieved to know he was safe, but talking to him made me miss him all the more. Since my entire family was an ocean away, I didn't have the luxury of leaning on my parents or my brother for support. I was on my own.

Thankfully, Porter and the men in his squadron all survived the many hours of combat patrol during Desert Storm, and I survived untold sleepless nights. But I will always remember that as a time filled with anxiety and even resentment for the price military families have to pay during war time, no matter how noble the cause.

Suddenly the phone began to ring, jerking me back to the present. First it was my dad saying that they had been advised to leave the office building for the rest of the day since it was the tallest building in the Tampa Bay area. It gave my mother some comfort to know that he was headed home. The next call was from my sixteen-year-old daughter, who had been watching the news on the televisions in her classrooms. She was upset and asked immediately if I had spoken to her father. She knew he was supposed to be at the Pentagon on that day and was beginning to let imaginations of the worst fill her mind. I assured her that although I had not heard from her dad yet, the information was still coming in about all of this, the Pentagon was a massive structure, and I was sure he was okay.

She responded by saying, "Well, the Twin Towers were pretty big too, and look what happened to them!"

I could tell that she was really upset, so I asked her if she wanted me to come and pick her up. She said no, that she wanted to stay there with her friends for now and that it was okay for me to call her on her cell phone, which was something not normally allowed, once I heard from Porter.

After we hung up, I wondered if they were allowing the younger children at the middle school to watch the news and learned later that most had not been allowed to watch the coverage as some teachers felt it was too horrific for some of the children to absorb. I called the office of my son's school to make sure that things were under control there, and they responded that some parents had come to pick their children up and others had not. The majority of the children were not aware of what was happening, and the faculty was making every attempt to get through the day with as normal a routine as possible.

My mother had gone in to check on my grandfather and commented that he was still sleeping peacefully. We were grateful for that, as neither of us wanted to leave the living room where we were glued to the events as they unfolded. As time went on, we learned more about the plane that had hit the Pentagon. There were an unknown number of fatalities and scores of people who were badly injured. My heart was racing, and I said a silent prayer for Porter, hoping that he was not in the area that had been hit. All I could do was wait until I heard from him and try not to go mad in the process. I couldn't allow myself to even contemplate that after all the drama of worrying about Porter during the war, I could actually lose him right here at home in one of the safest buildings in our country.

We switched back and forth from CNN to FOX, desperate to glean any information we could. The phone rang again, and I raced to pick it up, desperate for it to be Porter.

It was my brother calling to check in with my parents. He asked after Porter right away and was alarmed to hear that he was at the Pentagon. I talked with Stewart for a minute but was too anxious to concentrate on anything but the TV for any length of time and passed the phone off to my mother.

Just then my cell phone beeped indicating that my battery was low, and I realized that I had not charged it the night before. Porter was usually the one that made sure our phones were plugged in at night, and since he was gone, I had overlooked it and was furious at myself. I was certain that if he tried to contact me it would be either on my cell or at my parents' house since he was aware of my plans to spend the day with my mother and my grandfather.

Hour after hour passed as we watched the destruction and the aftermath…it was unbelievable. There were a number of images I knew I would never be able to get out of my head. It was heart wrenching to see the fear on the faces of the people who ran for their lives down the streets of Manhattan, many of them covered with a layer of dust so thick you could barely tell if it was a man or a woman, let alone what race they were. Later that day as Mayor Rudy Guiliani stood before the cameras to address the stunned people of New York City, his words brought tears to my eyes. He said something to the effect that he was sure that when the numbers for the loss of life came in, it would be more than any of us could bear. And he was right.

As time wore on and I didn't hear from Porter, concern turned to absolute cold fear. I paced and paced. My dad had arrived home hours ago, which was a comfort to my mother. My children called and went home with close friends for the night, and my daughter made me promise to call the minute I heard from her father.

I was selfishly relieved that I didn't have to worry about the kids for the evening. My mind was filled with images of

Porter hurt or trapped. I tried to concentrate on the television, but the constant scenes of death and destruction were depressing me and increasing my level of anxiety as I worried about my husband and when I would hear from him.

Then finally around ten that night, the phone rang, and I was so beside myself with fear that I couldn't even answer it. I was still at my parents' house, and as I stood watching my father answer the phone with tears in my eyes, I feared the worst. I felt my knees go weak when my father handed me the phone and said simply, "It's Porter."

"Porter, Porter," I cried. "Are you all right? I've been worried sick."

As I stood there shaking, Porter said, "I'm okay, honey. I'm in a hospital in Virginia."

I felt relieved to know that he was okay enough to talk to me but terrified of why he was calling from a hospital.

"Oh no, Porter … are you hurt?"

Porter went on to explain that he had been near the area of the Pentagon that was hit, and that in the intervening chaos, which he would explain in more detail later, he had received first- and second-degree burns on his hands, arms, face, and the top of his head. I asked him if he was in a lot of pain. He said not more than he could manage and that considering his circumstances, he was fortunate to even be alive. He sounded tired and said that he would call again in the morning, and he would talk to me more then. He asked about the kids, and I said they were fine and told him that I loved him. I hung up the phone, thanked God that Porter was alive, and said a silent prayer for all the families who had lost loved ones because of this senseless tragedy.

As I turned to fill my parents in on Porter's condition, I saw my mother standing in the hall crying softly. My father had his arms around her. I rushed to assure her that Porter was in the hospital and was hurt, but that he would be okay.

My father looked up at me and gently said, "That's fine, dear. We're glad he is safe."

"Why is mother crying then?"

Before he could even answer, I realized that they were standing outside my grandfather's door.

"Oh no," I whispered. "Is he gone?"

My father nodded and said that he must have died quietly in his sleep within the last fifteen minutes because my mother had just been to check on him not long before Porter had called. I couldn't believe it; on this day in the midst of all the chaos of a world gone mad, my grandfather had quietly slipped away, never even knowing about the tragedy that rocked the world. As I walked into his room, he looked so peaceful, like he was sleeping. As I gently laid my head upon his chest for the last time, all the sorrow of the attacks and the fear and tension of worrying about Porter suddenly hit me, and I began to sob uncontrollably.

The emotions of that day were like one very long rollercoaster ride. I was so relieved to finally get word from Porter, only to learn that in the next room, my beloved grandfather had left this world like so many others had on that day. The sad and obvious difference was that my grandfather was in his nineties, had lived a good, long life, and knew that the LORD was going to call him home soon. No one in the Twin Towers or on those airplanes or working in the Pentagon knew that they had so little time left, that someone they had never met was deciding that they should die.

In those moments when hate made men blind, the world lost something. It realized once again that men whose hearts have become hardened can put aside all feelings of compassion for their fellow human beings. They can act without reservation, without remorse for the death and destruction they know they are about to release upon innocent people.

It was with a heavy heart that I called my children to tell them the news that their father was safe but that their beloved great-granddad had died. My eleven-year-old son, who by then was aware of the events of the day, commented that heaven was sure busy greeting people today. And for the first time all day, I smiled.

We said good-bye to my grandfather on a windy, rainy Florida day, with one eye on a slowly approaching hurricane. It was a small service; we had told most family and friends not to risk getting out in the weather, and some had already left ahead of the storm.

I sat looking out the window that lined one entire wall of my grandfather's room at the funeral home. As the rain pounded furiously and the wind blew the palm trees sideways, I marveled at the circle of life. No matter who is born or who dies, life goes on. The sun will continue to rise and set, the days will follow on, one after the other, and slowly but surely, broken hearts will mend.

After we laid my grandfather to rest with full military honors, my thoughts turned to Porter—I was anxious to get to Virginia to see him. In the past few days, I had learned more about how he received his injuries. He and an old friend, Colonel Derek Jacobs, had been taking a tour of a newly refurbished area of the Pentagon when the plane hit. Porter and Derek made it out alive through a terrifying maze of smoke and fire. But this was only after they had rescued a young army first lieutenant, Nancy Jo Swenson, who had been showing them around and was in her sixth month of pregnancy.

In her panic after the attack, she had crawled to the nearest room she could find and hid underneath a heavy desk. By the time Porter and Derek found her, she was unconscious, curled up into a fetal ball in a desperate attempt to protect her unborn child, and the desk she was under was on fire. As Derek grabbed a chair and tried to clear the burning debris and make a path to the window, Porter made one last attempt to get the girl out from under the desk. As he finally got her free, the desk collapsed on both of them, burning Porter's arms, hands, and the top of his head. Derek cleared the debris off them, severely burning his hands, and he and Porter managed to get the girl passed through the window into the unknown arms of another man in uniform who had run to the building to offer help.

Porter and Derek fell into a heap together as they jumped out of the window with a wall of flame and black smoke licking at their heels. They were both rushed to the hospital, and on the day of my grandfather's funeral, Porter learned that the young first lieutenant they saved had survived, and so did her son, who was born three months later and was named Porter Derek Swenson.

On September 11, 2001, for one brief moment in time, darkness had its say. But always, always behind the darkness, there is light. And in those days after the terrorist attacks on America, stories of goodness, bravery, selflessness, and compassion quietly took their place beside the many tales of horror and grief. People witnessed the worst that man can do and responded with acts of kindness and love, showing the best that man can do. It should be the hope of all people whose hearts have not been hardened and filled with hate that the latter show of human emotion will have a more lasting impact than the former.

As a military wife whose husband continues to do his part to fight terrorism, wherever that may take him, I will try to do my part to ensure that those people who gave the ultimate sacrifice of their lives are not forgotten and that their families aren't forgotten. Wherever there is terror, sadness, or pain, let it be us, proud and strong military wives, who help to bring love where there is hate, compassion where there is need, companionship where there is loneliness, and light where there is darkness. Let us do this with the strength of a lion and the gentleness of a lamb, and let the healing begin.